D1286580

Blumenberg

THE GERMAN LIST

SIBYLLE LEWITSCHAROFF

Blumenberg

TRANSLATED BY WIELAND HOBAN

LONDON NEW YORK CALCUTTA

This publication was supported by a grant
from the Goethe-Institut India

Seagull Books, 2017

Sibylle Lewitscharoff, *Blumenberg* © Suhrkamp Verlag, Berlin, 2011
English Translation © Wieland Hoban, 2017

ISBN 978 0 8574 2 369 6

British Library Cataloguing-in-Publication Data
A catalogue record for this book is available from the British Library

Typeset by Seagull Books, Calcutta, India
Printed and bound by Maple Press, York, Pennsylvania, USA

For Bettina Blumenberg

CONTENTS

The Lion I

Blumenberg had just picked up a new cassette to put into his recorder when he looked up from his desk and saw it. Large, yellow, breathing; undoubtedly a lion. The lion looked over at him, it looked over to him calmly as it lay there for the lion was stretched out on the Turkmen rug, not far from the wall.

It must have been an older lion, perhaps no longer in possession of its full strength, but gifted with the unique power to be there. Blumenberg could see that, at least at second glance, while still making an effort to control himself. 'Don't lose your composure, least of all now,' Blumenberg told himself; perhaps the sentence came out less correctly, although Blumenberg normally maintained an iron discipline even when finding the right words in his head, as he had grown used to putting sentences together in an orderly fashion, not impetuously, almost as orderly as the way he usually spoke, whether he had a primed recording device or a child in front of him.

Blumenberg immediately knew that he could take many wrong courses of action here, but only one right one: to wait and keep calm. He also knew that he was being awarded a great honour in the form of the lion, as if an honorific message of a lofty nature had been delivered, prepared long in advance and granted to him after thorough consideration. Someone evidently felt that Blumenberg, at his somewhat advanced age, could handle this with ease.

The only curious thing was that there was nothing unclear or hazy about it, nothing resembling a mixture of lion and air atoms; its outline did not tremble with the back and forth of Blumenberg's swirling thoughts; there were no lion-headed mirror neurons flashing up and teeming through the crystalline shimmer of a hallucination. The lion was there. Hearty, furry, yellow.

Though he admonished himself to be an imperturbable model of calm, his heart was racing: A lion! A lion! A lion!

He was not afraid of it, of course. It did not look like a runaway circus lion. For one thing, Blumenberg was shielded by the large, heavy desk behind which he was sitting, and for another, this lion was lying there utterly calm, behaving not at all like a distressed escaped animal, let alone a nervous eater of Christians. Blumenberg felt like saying, 'I am a Catholic, you can go ahead and eat me,' but kept his flippancy to himself and then, with an expression that was meant to signal expectant politeness, but ended up conveying a little too much curiosity, he gazed at the lion. Perhaps the way he was looking at the lion would have an inciting effect, Blumenberg thought, for he was aware of his burning gaze.

The lion's beer-coloured eyes surveyed him unwaveringly with all their lion's calm, which is to say, they did not really survey him so much as look through Blumenberg at something behind him, perhaps behind the bookshelves, perhaps behind the wall of the house, or behind Altenberge and the town of Münster in 1982, in a time far away.

His heart was still pounding like a little machine out of control.

Conversing with a lion was not something Blumenberg had practised. After all, there had never been an opportunity to do such a thing. Blumenberg had always found it easy to speak to his beloved Axel, the white-haired collie. Axel had followed his every footstep, and it had been a pleasure for Blumenberg to run his fingers through the long, thick fur, and tickle its neck, while speaking to it very naturally, almost like a childish lover mad with affection, albeit—compared to other dog-lovers—remarkably correctly.

Blumenberg had his doubts that a conversation with the lion would even be possible. It was out of the question for him to stand up, stroke the lion's mane and give it a good ruffling. The lion did not seem in need of any affectionate gesture whatsoever. Though Blumenberg was not afraid, he felt great respect for the animal.

The lion has come to me because I am the last philosopher who can appreciate it, Blumenberg thought to himself. At this thought he was overcome by a queasy feeling; he had to close his eyes for a moment, faced with so much greatness placed on his carpet by some nonchalant hand, a challenge from the night—late at night, at quarter past three, as a glance at the clock revealed when he opened his eyes again.

Nether a smell nor an absence of smell emanated from the lion; the lion smelt discreetly of lion, perhaps just enough to be identified by the nose of one who loved lions, and made an effort to recall the lion's smell after a visit to the zoo. Blumenberg could certainly claim to be a lover of lions but the smell of lions had never been of concern to him. The sharpness of the odour that began to fill his study, which was bold, yet no more than a trace floating upwards, wafting in and vanishing again from one breath to the next, aroused Blumenberg's senses.

Thoughts accosted him forcefully, with a vividness he had never known; it was as if all the drawers of his safe had flown open and the thirty-six thousand, six hundred and sixty typed index cards kept in them were flying out as if in a fountain, though not in their actual paper form, but as little pictorial surfaces separated from the letters and notes, pushing their way into his head.

Quiet please. Keep a clear head. One can only get to the heart of a picture, the heart of a problem, if one calmly lays out and examines the individual picture, the individual problem. Who was the lion? Because he was attempting to build up a defence against the flood of images, Blumenberg felt slightly frenzied.

Agave's false lion. The fable of the lion's court. The psalmist's lion, roaring. The lion forever vanished from the Land of Canaan. The symbolic animal of Mark the Evangelist. Mary of Egypt and her lion companion. The pious animal of Saint Jerome in his study. Who was the lion?

His memory should scour the Bible at high speed, for that was where the lion's telltale fangs, attached and broken off again, were located; Blumenberg gave himself this order. But he had to admit that now of all times, his memory, which normally functioned perfectly, better than that of anyone he knew, was not up to a thorough examination of the lion problem.

Although only a few moments had passed since the animal's appearance, Blumenberg had already built up trust in it; and yet there was no way of telling what kind of relationship would develop between them, whether it would last or not. How amazing that I already find myself hoping our relationship could endure, Blumenberg thought. For a moment he imagined that the lion, whose jaws were very slightly open, was smiling.

Its age? The lion was old, ancient even, surely older than a lion would ever grow in the wild. Blumenberg noted it with regret. The animal's mane—it had probably been majestic in its early and middle years, but now it seemed tattered. Its spine was visible and sagged slightly, and large, dark tear channels led from the lion's eyes to the side of its face; the very way it breathed, its stomach contorting each time as if with a little spasm, was already disconcerting.

Surely the lion has not come to die on my carpet, Blumenberg thought with dismay. Someone up there wanted to have a joke at his expense and had sent him this poor excuse for a lion for that purpose. The thought vanished again as quickly as it had seized him. No, Blumenberg was sympathetic to the lion, and the moment he admitted this to himself, he trusted in the enlightening power of sympathy. All of a sudden he felt wrapped in a homely self-warmth, a feeling that differed only slightly from self-exaltation. He was the exemplary ascetic who had earned his lion. Working night after night after night, Blumenberg told himself proudly, the thanks had now come in the form of the lion.

It was impossible for him to feel like Mary of Egypt. The desert was missing, as were the excesses and revelry in which this very particular Mary had once indulged, and naturally the turnaround. Blumenberg had never indulged in such bodily extremisms, had not needed to turn around, and was not a woman. Nor did the thought of lying in the desert, with dried-up bones and a lion above him guarding his grave, appeal to him.

Agave? Nonsense! Mistaking one's own son for a lion and tearing him to pieces in a bacchanalian delirium—only a woman who had sprung up in wild Greece could be induced to do such a thing, or more precisely woman in her heightened form: the ancient mother.

Although the lion spread out in front of him was certainly not a dream and its broad-nosed head was undoubtedly genuine, and not secretly that of a cat, for instance (and this lion was also looking further and further through him), a peaceful study-feeling gradually overcame the philosopher. He called to mind the famous copperplate by Dürer. Admittedly his room, Blumenberg's, lacked the hourglass with sand running through it, it lacked the book-rest, it lacked the crown-glass windows and the skull on the windowsill, and instead of the warm wooden panelling there were bookshelves and carpets extending to the ceiling; but it was a retreat nonetheless, stupendously secluded from the rest of the house. In addition, it was night. Those hours of radical withdrawal from the world's busyness in which a handful of sleepless souls, at most, tossed and turned, and only very few people carried out their duties.

In spite of this, Blumenberg began to have doubts. If he now closed his eyes very firmly and counted to sixty— he had become used to performing such counting with a tiny twitch of his fingers—and then opened them again, the lion might disappear. An illusion, nothing more.

Blumenberg did indeed close his eyes, yet in his confusion he counted not to sixty but accidentally only as far as fifty-eight, finding it very hard to keep his eyes pressed shut for so long.

Eyes open. The lion was there.

Blumenberg began to feel like leaving his place behind the desk. The moon was shining outside. The black skeletons of the rosebushes showed themselves in front of the drawn-out windows. Perhaps he should open one side of the window, just to get everything out into the open.

Might the lion, for all its apparent benignity, do something to him? Was it dangerous to turn his back on it? Blumenberg wondered. He got up from his chair as if in slow motion, walked halfway around his desk and slowly, far more slowly than usual, went to the window.

Dangerous? No, evidently not. For a few seconds, Blumenberg stood at the window and breathed in the cool night air, albeit with his back tensed. When he turned around again, the lion was still there.

Time to open a bottle of Bordeaux. The event, the appearance of the lion, called for a celebratory drink of wine. With his glass filled, Blumenberg remained alone; it would have been futile to look for a guest glass in his study. The lion was not, after all, quite so domesticated that it could hold a glass in its paw and raise it to Blumenberg's health.

The lion, which, it seemed to him, had now lowered its head slightly, but still looked through him unmoved, covered sixteen, seventeen—or nineteen?—elephant feet on the Turkmen rug, which was one of the few possessions he had inherited from his father. In choosing this warming surface to lie on, it had behaved like a house dog. 'It has a sense of symmetry,' Blumenberg thought, as the lion had lain down more or less exactly in the middle, 'and it seems to have a sense of aesthetics too.' The rug was the most valuable object in Blumenberg's study, with dabs of light colour against a ruby background and blue-green-black gradations—truly an exquisite piece.

Though there was nothing wrong with his study, Blumenberg was sorry not to have as glorious a room at his disposal as the one painted by Antonello da Messina. The painting, which the Italian master had laid out with strong shadows in the Dutch style, was now recalled by Blumenberg's memory, working perfectly again, with fabulous precision: the viewer gazes through a stone opening, with a peacock, a copper bowl and a quail on the parapet. In the splendid interior, a miniature stairway with one, two, three Trinitarian steps to a dais. The saintly scholar in flowing red velvet robes and a red velvet cap, leafing with his long arms through a book that lies open before him on some form of desk with a slanted front. On the left a magical view out of the window: a hilly landscape with scattered cypress trees. And on the right, behind the scholar's dais, emerging from the darkness, a scrawny lion. No, not with lion's legs and broad paws, but equipped with thin, short racing legs like a greyhound. Antonello had probably never laid eyes on a lion.

Blumenberg loved the painting. These dignified, lonely figures who made do with few books, evidently because they kept studying the same ones—above all the Bible, of course—again and again; their opulently-fitted rooms with the exquisite views of an orderly outside, presenting the solitude in a gloriously cosy light! The stage-like arrangement, the elevation of the visible side, served to remove the scholar from the tiled floor, this artfully squandered floor, as if he were less subject to gravity, as if his floor were not the ground of ordinary life, but that of the spirit from which his thoughts rose higher and higher. Was the learned hermit's red robe intended to indicate the elevation of his heart? What had not been painted, of course, was the draught that would have been blowing between the large opening at the front and the window cavities behind in the midday glare, sending the loose papers flying and spinning through the room. For a moment, Blumenberg imagined the comical lion as a paper-hunter, a paper-snatcher, but then immediately broke off the sentences that wanted to form to that effect, as he did not wish to lose himself in silliness.

Back to his own lion. Despite its remarkable appearance, which had only taken place half an hour ago, Blumenberg considered it advisable not to break his habits on any account—not even in this extreme situation, with his heart beating in his throat. The lion had already caused him such confusion that he had been unable to dictate the usual amount to his secretary; that was enough of a deviation from the norm. He packed the one full cassette in an envelope, not letting anything deter him—lion or no lion—from writing the address of the university on it clearly, albeit a little shakily, and putting a stamp on it. He reached for his coat and left through the garden gate, giving the animal an arresting look, as if he wanted to nail it to the carpet.

Outside he lit up a cigarette: this was another deviation, for he usually walked the distance to the letter box and back to the house at a stiff pace, and smoking would only have cost time. This time too he went excitedly through the sparsely lit streets—as usual there was no one about at this hour, and even the parked cars under the street lamps seemed asleep—but walked more slowly than usual to think over calmly, for a moment, by the night air, what had happened to him in the last hour.

I have been ambushed, he thought; someone has confronted me with a fundamental deception to test my mental powers.

When he returned, the lion was gone.

Blumenberg kept his hand for a long time on the handle of the garden gate, which he meanwhile closed. Had he been dealing with a fantastic lion, the *absent lion*, which was not part of what is the case, and hence never ever of the world? But, but, thought Blumenberg, this completely different, world-rejecting lion does occur *in something* and is thus, in a new and different way, *the case*. The language games of the world-namers bring the lion back into existence and life, he mumbled quietly to himself.

Satisfied with the term 'world-namer', which he immediately applied to himself, Blumenberg went to bed.

Coca-Cola

As usual, Blumenberg awoke around half past eleven. All he could remember of his dreams was that his father had given him an African postage stamp bearing a motif of a lion with an upturned tasselled tail. The stamp had been given to him with a pair of tweezers, changing in slow motion from the father's large hand to the child's. No, not quite. A dream paralysis befell him: the movement came to a halt, his child hand could not grasp the tweezers, and this frozen state worked the dreamer up so intensely that he awoke, but immediately went back to sleep.

Nonetheless, he had drawn a tremendous amount of consolation from his sleep; he had rarely felt so good, and even had the urge to hit a ball over a tennis net again—quick, quick—the way he used to, now tentatively raising his arms to chest height and pushing his elbows back. He had not felt such thirst for action in years. He felt a tingling sensation in his legs, a hunger to chase after a ball; he saw clouds of red dust being kicked up and heard the bright plop when the racquet hit the ball, as well as the darker sound when the ball went flying into the sand. He asked himself whether it had truly been a wise decision to lead the life of an extreme homebody with rusting bones. Just then he felt a twitch of pain in his left leg, in the exact place where he had once pulled a muscle after diving after a ball unsuccessfully and hitting the ground.

Before drinking his first coffee, taking off his dressing gown and clothing himself for his daily business, he looked for the lion in his study. No lion anywhere. Which was not especially surprising, for it was a bright day, a radiantly bright day in May, when everything was shining as if it had just been made and only tangible things stepped into the light.

The half-empty wine bottle and the glass were still standing there. Blumenberg's nostrils widened; after he had wandered back and forth sniffing a few times, it seemed to him as if there were still a residual odour of lion hanging in the room. He opened two windows and stared at the bee-filled rosebushes.

His lecture today dealt with the human need for consolation and the simultaneous incapacity for consolation. He entered the hall in Münster Castle punctually at quarter past two through a side door. The seating rows were packed, just filling up with the last few latecomers. Blumenberg's eye fell upon the lectern; his face revealed disgust. Six empty Coca-Cola bottles were standing there to mock him. Whether placed there intentionally or left unintentionally, they stood there as a provocation. Blumenberg took off his coat and Homburg hat, placed his bag on the long counter that enclosed the lectern on both sides, and considered what he should do. He would not waste a single word on it. To avoid direct contact between his skin and the sticky object as far as possible, he picked up the first bottle with the tips of his thumb and forefinger and carried it to the windowsill on the courtyard side.

'The human need for consolation is profound,' Blumenberg said in a slightly nasal voice while turning around, strolling to the lectern and doing the same with the second bottle as he had with the first: 'The efforts undertaken by humans to console humans are immense, but rarely successful.'

An incredible suspense built up in the venerable hall, but no one dared laugh.

He spoke slowly and with cutting precision: 'With questionable justification, the need for consolation and the capacity for consolation are placed under the protection of a certain embarrassment, rather like poverty or stupidity. Discrimination against consolation progresses inexorably.'

In the meantime, he had reached the third bottle and performed its removal so evenly that he even took the same number of steps for each journey back and forth: exactly twenty-two.

Holding the body of the fourth bottle with his fingertips, he elaborated: 'Consolation rests on the general ability of humans to delegate, on the fact that humans do not have to do and carry everything that behoves them and devolves upon them on their own.

But,' said Blumenberg, and with this 'but' he took the fifth bottle, 'we have become incapable of using the tremendous arsenal of instruments for consoling and contenting that has accumulated in the history of mankind.'

'This applies most of all to interpretations of the world, whose only function is to offer humans consolation.' As he returned from transporting the sixth bottle, he spoke as energetically as if he had to etch his definition into the brains of his listeners with a graver: 'All suspicion towards consolation, all defamation of needs for consolation, rests on the assumption that it is an avoidance of consciousness.'

He opened his briefcase and took out a bundle of index cards and a few pages of manuscript, spreading them out on the counter with complete calm. 'You, ladies and gentlemen, are beings that need consolation, sometimes even real sissies, and I am the same; we want to console and be consoled, but things are not quite so simple.'

As he looked up from his cards, he saw it. The lion came trotting down the centre aisle, not in a dead straight line, but swerving slightly back and forth as big cats do. It approached just as Aristotle had described it—with powerful, wiry legs, a broad shoulder girdle, a sound ribcage and back, rocking its shoulders as it walked. This lion was significantly younger than he remembered it, a stately specimen of a lion in full possession of its powers and demands, covered in a fully intact, shining coat of fur.

'When the consoler comes,' Blumenberg rejoiced to himself, 'we may not recognize him.' It was clear beyond any doubt that the lion went unrecognized. The listeners in their seats did not see it. Blumenberg continued unwaveringly: 'The programmes of consciousness to which we have devoted ourselves, the constant urgings to become more consciousness—they force us to make our decisions in accordance with realism. The overbearing irruption of things into our words robs us of the ability to give consolation, to receive consolation.'

For all its stateliness, the lion in the hall seemed smaller than the lion in the study.

He explained, 'To the extent that humans constantly force one another to follow realism, they are as much in need of consolation as ever, but in real terms they are inconsolable. They have abandoned the reign of wishes and the capacity for illusions, and thus deprived themselves of a wide range of consolations that could free them from the frightening entanglement of becoming and fading.'

Blumenberg did not believe a word of what he had just said. The lion refuted him with aplomb. It exuded a strong aura of consolation. It had come to rest slightly to the right of the counter; quite a picturesque sight, Blumenberg thought. For a moment he saw himself as a little man and the lion as gigantic; lying comfortably between the lion's paws, Blumenberg gave his lecture. Hanging over his tiny human head was the commanding head of the lion, whose occasionally exposed teeth added urgency and edge to everything that was mentioned in the lecture.

The lion turned its head towards Blumenberg, but could also have turned it to the students and thus looked across the hall, an old lecture hall that sloped upwards slightly, with windows that almost went down to the floor on both sides. Those seated in the rows were not only young students, however; an educated older audience from the city, including a number of professors from other departments, regularly attended Blumenberg's lectures. In the front row were some particularly eager students who were pointing the microphones of their cassette recorders towards him.

They all looked straight through the lion, as if it were indistinguishable from the wooden floor. Four young people sitting scattered around the hall, however, felt that something extraordinary had happened, something beyond their professor's book-worthy performance with the Coca-Cola bottles. It was as if they had smelt something, detected it with fine little sensor hairs, that did not usually belong in a lecture hall. Richard, more hanging than sitting in the third row from the back with outstretched legs, was gripped by it as powerfully as Isa, who—as always—was sitting as straight as a pole in her first-row seat, slightly to the right of the lectern; Gerhard and Hansi, spread out to the left and right at the middle level, were also infected by it, but none of them could have said what it was. Only Isa noticed that the professor was often looking down at the floor, at a point where there was nothing else to be seen.

A current of power flowed from the lion, filling Blumenberg with immense vitality.

He felt one with his skill as never before. To be sure, most of his lectures had turned out well. Lifting one's own person into a cultural sphere and letting it grow there by capturing a stream of thought precisely in the spoken word, transforming the abundance of favourable thoughts resulting from the enjoyment of others (mirrored in the attentive faces of his listeners) into self-enjoyment—he had long been familiar with all those things. Building up an elastic speech freely from one card to the next, which he pushed back and forth on the counter as in a game of solitaire, while alternately looking at the green park on his left and turning his gaze to the listeners again, sprinkling in a few jokes and breaking new ground that only revealed itself to him while he spoke, his memory never letting him down, rather integrating references and reflections vividly into this new ground—he was well-practised at this, he was a master.

He was aware of his extraordinary abilities. His professional skill as an appointed philosopher shone forth.

With his eye on the lion, he spoke animatedly. Spoke of sphere harps, pilgrim's hymns, the cosmos's desire to become, and a little miscellaneous news item about an American who had invented a time cap that looked somewhat like an embroidered tea cosy; nonetheless, it was meant to enable its wearer to feel their way into the world before birth and after death. He gathered such momentum in the course of this that he placed the imaginary time cap of Douglas E. Bickerson on his head with his hands raised.

To curb the spreading waves of merriment, he drew his next statement from the depths of his arched chest: 'Consider the temporal balance of humans, the most vulnerable point of their existence—consider how difficult it is to bring effective consolation to this irreplenishable finitude and irretrievability. To draw something completely unfamiliar into the familiar requires cunning artifice, and that may include a cap which resembles an embroidered tea cosy.'

Laughter in the hall. Blumenberg had gripped the higher of the side walls with both hands, now he removed them and placed them in parallel on the surface of the lectern: 'The tricks for extending time, transforming time, the wishes to return home to archaic irresponsibility, salvific plans of a higher kind and the mental forces that help these to succeed—all of that next time.'

He pushed the index cards together; while the audience rapped their knuckles vigorously on their seats in applause, he knocked his pile of cards into shape and returned them to his case, packed his hat and coat, and disappeared as quickly as he had come through the side door. Actually, not quite as quickly. Richard, Gerhard, Hansi, Isa and a few others observed a strange spectacle as their professor, having unlatched the door, suddenly paused and turned around and waited for a while, looking in front of him. As if to let someone pass, the man stepped politely aside, then turned around with an elegant swing, gripped the door handle, closed the door and was gone.

As always, he had not offered the attendees any opportunity for conversation after the lecture. It was simply not his style to linger around, on the lookout for some remark or other, perhaps a compliment or a foolish comment one of the students still wanted to share with him. He immediately entered his Peugeot and drove to the philosophy department, just a few metres away.

When he reached his office to be present for an appointment which a student had requested in writing, the idea that had rushed about inside him upon the lion's first appearance returned: the idea that it was all a student prank. At the moment there was no lion to be seen. Blumenberg was alone in the room.

A jape? But how could they have carried it out? His students were supposed to have brought a stuffed lion to Altenberge? And one that, as had just been proved, could also move completely naturally? Impossible. When he thought of his students, which he seldom did these days, he could barely recall a single one by name. Gone were the days when the new professor in Giessen would spend the afternoons and some evenings having animated discussions with assistants and students, wrapped in cigar and cigarette smoke and fuelled by wine and liqueurs. Gone the days of being a young whippersnapper who would contradict many an older colleague politely, but with hints of sardonic presumption—for example, Joachim Ritter, whom he had involved in an amusing discussion on the circulatory problems resulting from the upright gait of humans at a lecture by a physiologist at the Mainz Academy. He, Blumenberg, had questioned the advantages of two-leggedness as opposed to four-leggedness, implying in a clever, well-packaged, well-hidden and extremely discreet manner that the much-vaunted upright gait of humans was not as impressive as all that—in the metaphorical sense too, as shown by the experiences of recent German history.

But he had long since withdrawn from such tumults. Instigating discussions to make himself heard, to display his brilliance, were a thing of the past. Naturally the odd student still aroused his interest nowadays; there was that girl in the first row, for example, who always sat in the same place and followed his every gesture as if spellbound. Bit by bit, however, he had lost that interest in the students which he had felt—and very keenly so—in his early teaching years.

Today he was to see a certain Gerhard Baur. There was a knock at the door at quarter past three, exactly on time, and a tall, thin person entered. Blumenberg remembered that the young man had come to see him before, and had made a favourable impression. On the first visit he had had been reminded of Reinhold Schneider, another beanpole, some six and a half feet tall, who had always stooped in order to undo the twenty or so centimetres of excess height.

The young Baur was certainly less melancholy than the poet had been; his open face, with its red cheeks and hair that hung like a pageboy's, stirred paternal feelings in Blumenberg. He also had jug ears, pert listening organs that broke out through his smooth brown hair as little rosy discs.

Blumenberg asked him to take a seat at the small round table, in one of the low armchairs reserved for visitors, and sat down next to him. From the window one had a direct view of the cathedral square. Blumenberg resided on the cathedral hill; his room was modest, but not withdrawn. Neither of them cast a single glance at the cathedral.

Baur did not beat about the bush explaining the reason for his visit. He was quite overwhelmed by Blumenberg's knowledge, he professed and smiled bashfully, he could take in, at most,10 per cent of what Blumenberg offered in his lectures, probably less, and yet he wanted to embark on a comparative study of some of the most famous ancient and biblical heroes—Hercules, Perseus, Mopsus and Samson—of whom Samson, the one betrayed by all women, and who could express himself so poetically, was particularly dear to him. It was for this that he was seeking Blumenberg's advice.

As far as the 10 per cent were concerned, the professor reassured him that even the most inquisitive person could only absorb and work with those ideas that could be integrated into their own cosmos of thought at that particular time. He found Baur's subject worthwhile; he saw particular promise in the comparison between Hercules and Samson as outlined somewhat tentatively by Baur, but with a flicker of flames around his words. Blumenberg lost himself in thoughts of the Jewish muscleman's massive stature and his seven locks; fulfilling God's salvific plan trembling, lonely and torn by passions, much about him was childlike—the childishness of the sweet-toothed gourmand, for example, who scooped honey from the lion's skeleton with his bare hands.

Blumenberg now returned to something from which he had usually kept his distance in recent years: he encouraged the student to write to him about the progress of his work, assuring him support in the form of advice and comments.

The little discs of Baur's ears were glowing with joy as he carefully pressed the door handle of the office and closed the padded double doors behind him quietly, very quietly, as if to avoid waking an infant.

Blumenberg felt good. The modesty of the young man, his eagerness and the intelligence that sometimes flashed in his turns of phrase were proof: what he taught was not all in vain after all. Some of it landed in the receptive ears of a student, germinated and bore surprising fruits. He caught himself entertaining the idea of stroking young Baur's head to look after him.

He left the building shortly afterwards. Today he felt like walking, rather than getting in his car immediately for the trip to Altenberge. For it was a splendid day with that warmth of early evening, not hot and not too cool—ideal weather for a stroll. He decided to go for a short walk along the river Aa. Late spring had brought out all the leaves in perfection; barely any skeletonized by cater-pillars or bent, or dust-coated around their stems. The breeze was rustling the trees, whose branches seemed to be waving. The damp flowerbeds glowed pink, white, red and lavender. Two lost ducks waddled across the steamy lawn. He stopped, engrossed in the observation of a brown tulip; with a very straight stem and its head gracefully aloft, it stood all alone amid its colourful sisters, which had grown together in a crooked and cheerful tangle.

The sight of its furry stamens, intense black and resplendent, accompanied him for a few more steps before it gradually faded. On the way, he looked back several times. Was the lion following him? No, there was no sign of the lion. What if his family learned of the lion's existence? Not from him, for he would not breathe a word about it. But his wife, his daughter and his sons were clever, by no means insensitive when it came to important things that were happening around him; who knew, per-haps they would at least pick up the lion's smell. He laughed at the thought that the members of his house-hold would now put out gigantic portions of meat for the lion every day, serving them in an oversized dog bowl. On the other hand, this very special lion had probably gone without any meat for centuries.

It was imperative that he found out whom the lion was previously associated with, whom it had served before. With meat? Without meat? Without meat, Blumenberg decided. The trick of the lion was precisely that it existed without devouring the appropriate portion of meat like its brothers in nature. It appeared and vanished without leaving any trace, and did not even have to wipe away the paw prints with the tassel of its tail to prove its allegorical proximity to Christ (which would have been impossible anyway, whether in his study or the lecture hall); it did not have to show the whole world that it was doing something similar to Christ, who had repeatedly concealed the divinity of his human form. His lion left neither its excrement nor its fur on the carpet, at least not in 1982, not in the city of Münster on this fair day in May, which was now gradually covered by the twilight that ended it.

The Lion II

On the way to the car park, Blumenberg passed the sculpture by Ulrich Rückriem that rose from the grass and had stirred up much resentment, and was still doing so. Blumenberg found the slabs, which had a straight front and a sloping back, simulating rock walls placed side by side, quite superfluous; his anger was not, however, so great that he would have issued a public statement. As the slabs were constantly being defaced and then cleaned, it was impossible for the moss to cover the unfortunate sculpture from all sides and put it in a state of greenish approximation. Otherwise, in rainy Münster, the moss would have done a thorough job by now.

There was no lack of ghastly sculptures in the city. The ugliest monument was the status of Count von Galen, the 'Lion of Münster', who had fought from the pulpit against the euthanasia programmes and the machinations of the Secret State Police in the Third Reich. A stately man, a Westphalian giant with an imposing head and thunderous voice who did not put up with nonsense and, as early as 1934, had attacked the new rulers in an

Easter letter for their ungodly thoughts and actions. The man was firm, hard and tough as an anvil, an image he liked to invoke. The statue that was meant to represent him was awful. A kitschy, slimmed-down sculpture whose aesthetic came from the Nazi era; the artist had, however, smoothed out or omitted the muscles and everything else that had characterized the Lion of Münster. The figure stood on its pedestal in an impersonally bland straightness, a pitiful bugbear with its right arm raised in laughable fashion; one could certainly not have imagined it uttering so much as a peep against the machinery of death.

During the drive home, Blumenberg relished the lush green that still shone through the twilight in the valleys and meadows, contrasting with the black islands of forest. He was in good spirits and awaited the night.

The evening went as usual, the only difference being that he felt like having a decent portion of beef, and ate more of it than usual. Around nine, Blumenberg went to his study and was disappointed. No lion. He did the usual: read, revised the text he had written two nights previously, which had meanwhile been transcribed, made notes, pressed the 'record' button on the dictaphone and spoke the next part for his secretary. When he looked up from his papers in the middle of the dictation, the lion was back.

It was lying in the same place on the carpet as the previous night. Hearty, furry, yellow. It showed no instability of form that would have justified doubting its existence.

This time he felt an overwhelming urge to touch the lion, which did not seem at all averse to receiving a careful contact, hand to fur. Blumenberg was already on the point of getting up and walking over to it, but recalled the rule of *actio per distans* just in time and remained in his seat. Getting too close could destroy everything. The advantage of distance was that he could only presume to explore the commonalities between his mode of understanding and that of a creature trembling in the metaphysical, as well as the creaturely truth underlying both of them, at a suitable remove. Perhaps the possibility of truth as such was given for the first time now, by *not* touching the lion.

The lion had come to harbour him in its essence as no person ever had, and would ever be able to. On the other hand, it was regrettable that the lion had not shown any wildness, let alone readied itself to pounce on him. Otherwise he, Blumenberg, would have had to impose restraint on the lion as Saint Jerome did long ago, through eloquent persuasion and a well-composed attitude of devotion. Taming wildness through rhetoric and pious gestures! Blumenberg was annoyed that he had evidently not been thought suited to the slightest test of strength, but had to concede to himself that while he could have matched the church teacher when it came to rhetoric, he would never have managed to strike such perfect poses of devotion. Blumenberg had lost his faith, but not his love of the church.

The lion showed itself in its familiar aged form again. Had it fathered other lions in its youth? Only could hardly imagine it doing so in its tattered state. Blumenberg could not quite see his lion as the progenitor of little cubs that padded around their siblings, mewled, grumbled, lay bundled on top of one another and opened their jaws wide with relish.

He pressed the button on the dictaphone and spoke: 'Profound asker: What kind of lion is that? Flippant answerer: All lions are lions. Profound asker: Does that also apply to this special, slightly jaded-looking, perhaps excessively wished-for lion? Flippant answerer: One among many. Profound asker: Perhaps each one is different. Flippant answerer: All are different, yet one and the same.'

He paused. He felt like undertaking a peculiar experiment. Was the lion devoted to the truth? How would it react to a lie? Or to something improvised, some spontaneous offhand fairy tale? Blumenberg pretended to be speaking into his recorder but had not yet pressed the button, keeping an eye on the lion: 'Here, sitting on this chair, is a cobbler.'

No reaction from the lion.

Blumenberg hesitated for a moment and reflected. Then he spoke to his guest with a melodiousness that he found rather sultry: 'This is the story of an old, very old, in fact ancient lion that reappeared after centuries of slumber. As all eager children who read books about lions and visit them at the zoo know, a lion only lives six or at most seven years in the wild. Either a younger, stronger lion comes and kills it, or it is driven away and must wretchedly starve to death. Lionesses are better off; they stay in the pride and can reach an age of twenty years in the hunting community. At the zoo, of course, there is a possibility for a male lion to become quite old, and lions some in captivity even live for thirty years. But the lion of which I wish to tell lived,'—Blumenberg cleared his throat—'to a very, very old age.'

The lion yawned, displaying a few teeth.

He must have been too unctuous in his tone. Quietly, but insistently, Blumenberg continued: 'But the story of the lion, which is here being told not to the children but to the books, the desk and a yawning lion, which may only appear to be a lion, does not begin at the zoo but somewhere else. It begins in the desert. There, where everything is bone dry and all thoughts burn, at once clear and hard, a mound of sand began to stir: the old lion had awoken once more. It had raised itself and shaken the desert sand from its mane. After centuries, life had entered it again; it had risen to leave the desert and keep a significant man company.'

'This time, however, his visit would not be to a saint, but a philosopher. One might have thought that perhaps Ludwig Wittgenstein or Edmund Husserl—who could really decide on one?—or maybe even Friedrich Nietzsche's curved moustache would lure it from the desert, but no; it was a withdrawn philosopher in Münster, honestly doing his duty there as a university professor and yearning for the day when someone, with a swipe of a paw, would come and restore the context of the world; for his nightly activities consisted of philosophizing about its loss while simultaneously mourning for it.'

Blumenberg faltered. These tirades really made him feel quite foolish; he especially disliked the words 'withdrawn' and 'honestly'. The lion had only yawned once, and aside from that it had looked through him with the same placidity as before; but Blumenberg thought he had noticed little flames of irony glowing in its eyes. It had been a barely perceptible flickering, nothing more.

There was an awkward pause. Blumenberg had reached a dead end; he could not simply pretend that there was no lion there. The animal dominated his thoughts and feelings, and it made him nervous that the lion acted so calmly, or rather, did not act at all, and that its behaviour remained indifferent with regard to tests of truth, rhetorical fairy tale games or whatever else.

Blumenberg decided on an unusual course of action. He poured himself a glass of wine, stood up and sat cross-legged on the floor with his glass, roughly two metres away from the lion. The lion calmly accepted this advance. Indeed, Blumenberg had the impression that the lion was glad its roommate was no longer looking down on it, and was now almost on equal footing.

Blumenberg examined the light fur at the edge of the lion's belly and on the underside of its paws. For a moment he wished that the lion, in an act of playful submission, would roll onto its back and show its belly. Viewed at close quarters, it seemed even larger than from above. On the right side of its chest there was a long scar extending to the beginning of the front leg. Had the lion fought another lion for dominance in the pride? Despite the obvious blemishes of advanced age, a rather imposing mass had forced itself into visibility. The preservation of strength was enormous. Had a heightened will helped the lion to give itself the label of existence and remove it as it pleased? Or was the lion, however powerfully it might present itself, no more than a figment created by him, by Blumenberg, a man of intellect who was growing increasingly distant from the life led by everyone else, and who entertained the wish to have reality close to him, at knee-height, and in a reliably tamed form? Moderate, reduced in its drives, compact, not shattered into fragments—friendly?

Blumenberg recalled the word 'neuro-eccentric', which Thomas Mann had once used to characterize the medieval in their shared home town of Lübeck. Had he himself now become so neuro-eccentric that he imagined the lion not merely once or twice, but as an almost constant companion?

The wooden statue of Saint John hung on the wall above the lion—another object that had escaped his father's art shop at No. 6 Hansestrasse with only the slightest burn marks. Fine Art Publishers J. C. Blumenberg, Import & Export, Lübeck; the letterhead in brown writing appeared before his eyes for a moment. Saint John was holding an open book in his hands, immersed in its pages; he read unperturbed by everything happening around him, just as he had continued reading on Palm Sunday 1942 amid flying debris, covered in rubble and ash after an attack by the Royal Air Force. The lids of his pious eyes were lowered, lids into which tiny spikes had been carved to make them more dynamic. Despite the evangelist's concentrated pose, his clothes had a lively quality to them. It was as if restless winds had entered his robes from below, pulling them apart in some places and making them bulge in others. Perhaps John was murmuring words to the lion in order to keep its temper calm, finer words even than those he had written in his gospel, and only he, Blumenberg, was able to hear the murmuring.

At an angle above John, towards the left-hand corner, was a long crack in the wall. It had come about because the house was on a precipice and slanted downwards; the garden wall was no longer fully able to bear the load. Repair was out of the question, of course, for Blumenberg would have had to clear everything out and leave his study for weeks, maybe months—the very thought of it!

There was little doubt that the lion had no need for any a crack in the wall in order to emerge, and that the atmosphere had other tricks at its disposal for its disappearing and reappearing acts; and yet Blumenberg imagined that the irksome crack had now finally found its true purpose—the breath of the spirit was wafting in, with spirit beams groping their way through the crack into the room. He congratulated himself on being so obstinate and immediately cutting off every directly voiced thought of repairs.

Optatus

Gerhard had already become a glowing Blumenbergian as a schoolboy, at the Karlsgymnasium. Gerhard Optatus Baur, to use his full name. The missing *e** had made the surname unusual, taking it out of the rustic sphere and transforming it into something artificial, which lent the closing 'r' a particular emphasis and made it clatter like a little idling engine. On top of all that, his mother was infatuated with his eccentric middle name; she had welcomed the infant as desired and longed-for, in honour of a man who had almost always visited the canteen of the Württemberg State Library on Thursdays around half past twelve.

No, Eberhard Optatus Schneckenberger was not the father of little Optatus. By then, the scholar had been buried at Stuttgart Forest Cemetery for many years under a boulder from the Swabian Alps. He had held intellectual sway over the history of the region: its castles, palaces, city layouts, the regents, poets, philosophers, inventors

* The German word *Bauer*, also a common surname, means 'farmer'. [Trans.]

and engineers, the fruit tree culture, the rents, the wine, brandies, plague, religious confusion, and also the appearances by Goebbels at Cannstatt Sports Hall—in short, sway over the great narrative dough that swells up as regional history, and can be baked into a special construct of native dignity of which descendants are more likely than not to be proud. His services were also welcome at the *Stuttgarter Zeitung*, where he captured the attention of a loyal, by no means small readership with witty town stories, delighting them even as he lectured them.

Gerhard's mother worked as a cook at the State Library canteen, sometimes also as a cashier. She had positively seized the Thursday shift at the till after becoming aware of Schneckenburger and learning that he always came on the same day. Not that she was in love with him with every fibre of her being; the man was far too old for her, almost geriatric. No, she loved him for two shaky reasons stemming from the realm of vagueness: he was likeable and treated her respectfully. His thin, almost childlike scholar's figure, with skin that was still rosy in mature years, the white tuft of hair that stood up like a cockatoo's, and his trembling hands, which required considerable effort to find the right coins, filled her with a caring affection. He was such a clever chap! And he made royal quips about the slop that was slapped onto the plates with ladles from the stainless steel tubs.

Gerlinde Baur was an excellent cook; it pained her to see the slop served there on a daily basis, and she was inventive in at least upgrading the dishes with some seasoning. As far as the shopping and cooking procedures went, she was regularly at loggerheads with the head cook, but her protests fell on deaf ears.

Schneckenburger, at any rate, seemed to have recognized at first glance that a rather fine sort of person was sitting at the till. He soon began to wink at her while pushing the Thursday lentil and *spätzle* dishes and watery cucumber salad along the metal rails towards her, asking her at the same time to sprinkle a pinch of salt over the offering so that his taste buds and stomach would have an easier time of it.

Gradually the thing with the salt developed into a ritual between them. 'Could the mistress of the salt spare a pinch of her stock for me?' After a year or so he handed her a present: a pair of little salt and pepper jars made of blue glass, each in a braided silver basket from which fine threads extended to the perforated lid. For Gerlinde, it was the most beautiful present anyone had ever given her. Even on her deathbed at the Robert Bosch Hospital, to which she was sent by her cancer-ridden pancreas far too early, at the age of fifty-four, she asked her son to place the blue salt and pepper jars next to her in the coffin.

At first she had no idea who he was. When she heard two young fellows behind the old man poking fun at him with the phrase 'Optatus fright,' she asked a librarian and learnt the professor's full name. *Optatus*—these three syllables took her ears on a stroll.

Her son was born a few months after Schneckenburger's death, and she named him Gerhard Optatus.

Gerlinde heard something great, something optimistic and auspicious in the name. A little quill inside her seemed to be communicating with higher powers. The objections of her husband, who would have preferred a son called Fritz or Hans-Jörg, were of no importance. Gerlinde wished for her son to become a lover of books, a different type of person from her husband who spent day after day going upstairs and downstairs to read the private meters for the waterworks, then stepped into his camel slippers, and at weekends had little on his mind except the VfB Stuttgart. The man did not last long at Gerlinde's side, for he died at an even younger age than she did, a mere forty-one. This meant that Gerhard, who had no siblings but had his mother to himself for a time, was half-orphaned at the age of six and completely orphaned at twenty-one.

He turned out so light and his body so long.

Unlike most sons, Gerhard met his mother's wishes to a truly uncanny degree. The boy growing up on the second floor of No. 7 Tuchbleiche was not one of the usual Zuffenhausen guttersnipes. He learnt to read before he had even begun school, and was subsequently as insep-arable from his books as other boys from their footballs. He took them with him to bed, on the couch, to the kitchen table, in the tram or to the Berg spa. A clear can-didate for grammar school—a good one, with classics tuition. Gerlinde was only sorry that her little boy was growing so quickly. At thirteen he was already taller than his mother by a head and a half, and bent down when speaking to her. It was as if old Optatus had risen from the kingdom of the dead and let his educatory shadow glide over young Optatus; Gerhard became gentle and witty. It did not bother him in the slightest to be mocked for his name—on the contrary, he seemed to enjoy it. At school he was called 'Geges', a nickname that disappeared when he moved on to university. Although he had little physical power compared to his stronger classmates, despite his height, he was popular among them. Gerhard was clever, affable, useful for exams and easily persuaded to give up half of what little he had—for example, the artfully prepared sandwiches with a crispy crust which his mother put in his school bag every morning.

Gerhard already read Blumenberg's *The Genesis of the Copernican World* in his school days—without quite understanding it, admittedly, but with glowing enthusiasm and the secret satisfaction that he was probably the only person in Zuffenhausen to read it. Holding the book in his hands, he felt chosen. He had even spent his pocket money to buy the expensive clothbound edition, underlining so many passages with a sharp pencil and a little ruler, and adding so many exclamation marks in the margin that the lines showing through on the backs of those pages gave the book a strangely leaden, puffed-up appearance.

It was a matter of honour: Gerhard had to study with Blumenberg. After his A-levels he enrolled at the University of Münster, where his eye fell on Isa during a lecture in the first semester; for many weeks he contented himself with observing her from a distance, until—carefully, by indirect approaches, and standing with reddened cheeks at every encounter, not quite knowing what to do with his long arms and hot hands—he made her acquaintance.

So were they a couple or not? Difficult to say. Gerhard was certainly more in love than she was. It was his duty to look after the young woman, albeit discreetly. At the beginning, when they spent a few nights together in Isa's antique iron bed, things did not go smoothly; the experience did not give Gerhard an overwhelming urge to insist on any further bouts. What should one think of a woman who twirled his meagre chest hair between his fingers while whispering children's words to herself? He cursed the bedposts and rails. He had been pitifully trapped in that iron bed, tormented far more than usual by the length of his body, lying there with bent knees like a leaden Man of Sorrows and not sleeping a wink, feeling like a criminal because he had dared to force himself into the slender body of his beloved while she lay under him in a vacant state—and, to top it all, in a bed that was fifteen centimetres too short for him and had Patti Smith above it in a men's shirt, a jacket with a silver pilot's badge slung casually over one shoulder, looking down on him in what seemed like a disparaging manner.

Although he was normally relaxed about interacting with people, including those more intelligent or more attractive, Isa made him feel awkward. She had grown up in a different world and was accustomed to having her surroundings conform to her wishes. She came from

Heilbronn, where her father was a button manufacturer. Kurz & Sons, a company with a long tradition, famous for its vegetable ivory buttons, cherry stone buttons, horn buttons, mother of pearl buttons, engraved metal buttons, fabric- and leather-covered buttons, including hunting buttons—which could be opened and closed silently—and also yarn buttons, those old-fashioned fabric-covered buttons with star-shaped arrangements of threads; the hall was packed with complicated machinery for spinning, cutting, drilling, setting, shaping, claw chiselling, threading, smoothing, embossing and polishing, with a dedicated device for each material that was used to make the buttons.

Though not exactly pretty, there was something touching about Isa's slender form—the rapidly averted gaze, the fluffy chick hair, the childlike bosom and her childlike chubby hands, which did not quite match her thin little arms and always fiddled about somewhat agitatedly, for example when they were cutting bread in the kitchen and came within a hair's breadth of slicing into her flesh. Gerhard felt responsible for her, though he could not have said for what exactly. She had about five times as much money every month; she had a far-flung family that constantly checked on her well-being, she drove a midnight-blue Alfa Giulietta, had more acquaintances in Münster than he did and spent the holidays at her family's country estate in Mallorca, while he lived the life of an ordinary man, taking tinned peas out of cartons and stacking them on shelves.

Nonetheless, he considered himself a model of stability next to Isa. Though she was not frenetic, there was something flickeringly inconstant about her behaviour, and she was entangled in melodramas he could not decipher. Her frame of mind and body tension shifted rapidly between the sluggishness of someone stoned (in expectant trance) and an uncontrollable fidget; sometimes she became so weirdly absent and rigid that it seemed as if a stranger was sitting there. At such disturbing moments he feared that an inferno would erupt from within her, twisting her face into one great scream, but he had sufficiently strong nerves to refrain from asking what she was thinking. Gerhard had an acute sense of how one could become a nuisance to a person. In secret, he worried, pondering what was controlling the slim head of his girlfriend.

Blumenberg controlled it, that much was certain. At first Gerhard had thought it was mere trend-hopping, a dubious attempt to feel like one of the city's intellectuals, that led her to attend his lectures and effuse over them. But he soon realized that he was mistaken. Isa read Blumenberg's books with perhaps even greater zeal than he did, and she had an incredible memory for the way Blumenberg expressed himself, the gestures that accompanied his words, what suit and what tie he had worn, or how his hat was poised on his head. Sometimes she repeated Blumenberg's statements like a parrot, whether they fit into the context of a conversation or not: 'We know that we must die, but do not believe it because we cannot think it.' She grew angry if he likened Blumenberg's near-bald head to a polished egg head or ridiculed his entrance and disappearance through the side door as a *deus ex machina* gimmick. If he mentioned that Blumenberg was a family man with several children, she remained doggedly silent.

Isa began to speak in a strange way under Blumenberg's influence. She spiced her statements, which were normally much like the jargon of the young Münster students, with unusual words and turns of phrase. She no longer spoke of a shadow, for example, but of a 'shadow-cast', and referred to the grave as the 'repository cave', while a night was no longer a night but a 'Romantic recidive of the night'. None of this stopped her from listening time after time to *The River* by Bruce Springsteen or considering Grace Jones' steep hairstyle an important work of art. Naturally it angered her if one made fun of her for such discrepancies and called her a perfectly accounted-for Blumenbergian *pro memoria* item with questionable artistic judgement. But her anger quickly dissipated. He gazed, captivated, at her tight red pullover with a line of black rectangles running through the centre from top to bottom that bulged over her bosom.

It was also strange that Isa always wanted to sit in the front row and did not like it when he sat next to her. Her explanation was that she wanted to concentrate entirely on the lecture, and he would only disturb her. Well, he never liked sitting in the first row anyway. But it bothered him. His gaze was often drawn away from Blumenberg and wandered to her hair, and he found it bizarre that she sat there like a pharaoh for the almost two-hour lecture —Isa of all people, who normally slid about in chairs, ran her fingers through her hair, fiddled with the buttons of her shirts (she never wore blouses, only pullovers or men's shirts at least two sizes too large), twisted a scarf between her fingers and crossed one leg over the other in rapid alternation.

To a slightly lesser extent, Isa was controlled by another figure: Virginia Woolf. Gerhard was less concerned about her, as she was long dead and there was no danger that Isa would grovel ecstatically before her. Isa considered herself thoroughly 'Dallowayized', as she put it: everything happened at once around her and she vibrated with everything through energetic fingertip contact. It was difficult to know whether she was serious or only feigning, but she believed that her relationship with him, Gerhard, had an element of Mrs Dalloway's old love for Peter Walsh. The moment would come—only in a few decades, of course—when she had long since married and he would visit her after wandering long, very long, all over the world and break down in tears on her couch.

Gerhard could not imagine that quite so well, neither the wandering nor the tearful couch session. He had not wept since the death of his mother.

There was another bewitchment, however, that Isa kept strictly concealed from him; she did not breathe a word of it, not to anyone. While the fact that she was studying with an eminent authority by the name of

Blumenberg could still be vaguely reconciled with Patti Smith and Mrs Dalloway, two figures who embodied an attractive and eccentric way of being feminine across generations, the novel she read time and again to take its wasteful amorous opulence into her sleep and put herself in the place of the protagonist was, by the light of day—let alone of the reason taught by Blumenberg—not compatible with it. Isa was ashamed of her infatuation, nay, obsession. She was hopelessly bound to a novel, an unwholesome, even dangerous one at that. A novel whose kitsch vibrato seized her viscerally, yet which she would have vehemently decried if someone had mentioned it to her.

Everything that happened in *Her Lover* (*Belle du Seigneur*) by Albert Cohen was about her, with Blumenberg in tow. It was secondary that the novel was set in the 1940s, that the hero was a Jew who had lost all his connections, and that the woman he seduced was a demure, married, bored Swiss lady from an upper-class Calvinist milieu. Isa could claim the upper-class milieu, but not much more. In her flights of thought, she reworked everything until her love seemed identical to the novel: Blumenberg was a Jew, and in secret, erotically dangerous, a seducer with sparkling eyes bordering on the Luciferian, the sardonic, the knowing-every-trick, a verbal sorcerer who spoke in tongues, but who also spewed curses of abysmal depravity and despair—like Solal in the novel, who was sometimes a chameleon, sometimes a tattered elderly Jew and sometimes a radiant entangler of women, with opulent black curls. She masterfully overlooked the fact that Blumenberg's Judaism was a more complicated matter, not least through his Catholic baptism, but most of all, that Blumenberg was a family man with eccentric but iron-clad habits who would not hurl himself into any adventures, whether mindlessly or strategically.

How did the two dissimilar figures even become close? Although Isa enjoyed reading the first part of the novel, she could not quite integrate the seduction scenes into the framework of her own inner novel. Things started differently between them, only later reaching Cohen's heady pace—by now the scenes had gained such a hold on her that she not only relived them again and again while falling asleep but also in broad daylight, driving along the motorway in her Alfa, cycling in the city, sitting in a lecture or on a bench in the university park.

It was pouring with rain. Every time it was pouring with rain inside her head she desperately tried to stop the film, but no distraction could help her. Gerhard? Nonsense, not Gerhard. Gerhard was a lovely, clever chap, but she needed a man who would destroy her root and branch.

It was pouring with rain. She stood at the roadside soaking wet, holding a portfolio above her head. A Peugeot saloon drove past and then reversed, the windscreen wipers working frenetically—at first she could not tell who was sitting inside—and it was Blumenberg, the professor himself! He cranked down the right window and ask if he could help the *Fräulein* and drive her somewhere. She turned over the word *Fräulein* in her mind as she sat in the car; it was long since obsolete among young people, but from Blumenberg's lips it sounded enchanting in an antiquated way.

She sat freezing in Blumenberg's car. He handed her a jacket that had been lying on the back seat and covered her with it, and a conversation ensued in the dry interior, wrapped in torrents of rain, with the key phrase 'late-years lovers'—they were late-years lovers with heightened sensibilities for whom everything was possible. They agreed that love could attack and break down the defences of the modern caveman, but the shortest way to love was the only plausible one—naturally they both forgot their original destinations because they could not keep their hands off each other, and headed for a different city out-side of Germany (Isa's imagination had left it unspecified), and spent the night at an elegant hotel, and then—well, then everything developed much as it did in the novel: they were rootless, travelled from one hotel to the next, from the luxury hotels to the shabby dives, and wor-shipped their love, which became terrible and comprised theatrical gestures of rejection (on his part) and whim-pering submission (on her part), increasingly resembling more a drag show with cheeks painted red than the lofty school of love to which they had committed themselves when he placed the yoke of love on her and she willingly received it—until death entered the room, given by him first to her, then to himself.

Sunday

Gerhard inhabited two tiny chambers that were blazing hot in the summer and freezing cold in winter. They were located under the roof of a new five-storey building whose balconies were stacked on top of one another like halved octagons. His apartment had no balcony, however; instead there were hatches that could only be opened with brute force, as their frames had become warped. The house was seventeen years old, but the walls by the staircase were already decrepit. The layer of oil paint, once the colour of vanilla cream, was thoroughly wrinkled and flaking off. He refrained from inviting Isa there, although his two chambers were clean, at least cleaner than the rooms of Isa and her housemates. His apartment was crammed so full of books that one could almost forget the ill-conceived design, the ghastly woodchip walls and the ungainly plastic mounts on the windows and doors.

The small table at which he worked and ate, on which he placed newspapers and books, had been entirely cleared up except for a few typed pages, a pencil, a pencil sharpener in a Bakelite container and a cup. A thin-walled cup with a broad gold rim, elegantly curved inwards, used for both tea and coffee, on a saucer with the same gold border. Gerhard drank his coffee from this cup every morning—one of ten pieces he had taken with him after the liquidation of the household in Zuffenhausen.

It was not a children's magic cup that revealed a little bird on a branch or a landscape on the bottom once emptied; his mother had been attached to the cup, and he was attached to it too. When he drank his morning coffee from it, sadness flowed through his veins and nerves—only for as long as the coffee remained hot, and after that the sadness and his enjoyment of it dissipated. Gerhard loved this short-lived state. He needed his cup, and did not like to spend the night at Isa's apartment because he would have to forego it in the morning. It was laughable; he was acting like a little old aunt by making such a fuss over a piece of crockery, but he was sure nonetheless that the calm he needed for the day would flow to him in the morning from the bottom of the gold-rimmed cup.

That Sunday he did not know what to do. Lunchtime had already passed; he had stayed in bed for ages without sleeping. He was meeting Richard in the evening and did not much feel like working. The euphoria that had seized him while speaking to the professor and kept him awake for the last two nights had passed for now. He was befallen by his familiar Sunday paralysis, for he no longer went to church as he had during childhood and there was no festive lunch waiting for him. On Sundays he missed his mother's bustling. On Sundays he did not know what to do. It was already quite warm in his chambers; the apartment was beginning to develop its summer warmth Perhaps a little cycling tour?

Münster was so damned empty on Sundays. Calling Isa was out of the question—whenever he was in such a mood he sounded rather sheepish on the phone, which was poison for their relationship. It was even worse when one of her housemates answered the phone. Gerhard did not like those two, and they did not like him either. He was always given short shrift, and then the receiver made clicking sounds, evidently dangling carelessly from the wall.

The two of them seemed to have reserved Isa for themselves, or at least guarded her jealously. They did not seem to be lesbians, according to Isa, but he had never seen them in male company. He still felt the last Friday sitting heavily on his stomach. When he arrived, a feminist study group had just finished and the women were in high spirits—he already heard peals of laughter from the hallway, a storm of liveliness, which Gerhard listened to for a few seconds before ringing the doorbell. When he entered, however, he was met with abrupt silence: the women went past him to the door without a word of greeting, except for one, Hede, whom he knew from an art history seminar. She stayed in the hall for a while and chatted with him freely.

Isa was in a good mood that evening. She felt 'Dallowayized' again, joyfully at one with everything that crept and crawled, spoke, walked, stood and slept in the Münsterland. Portions of happiness were spent and handed out generously. 'Fear no more,' said Isa. At the moment he did not fear anything. The two were perched on their large Italian sofa, drinking Campari Orange and passing a joint back and forth. Isa wanted to know exactly what had happened at his meeting. For the first time, Gerhard had the impression that she admired him. With large, wonderfully shining eyes, her hands clasped around her drawn-up knees, she followed his description, enquiring as to every minute detail so that she could absorb everything about the precious conversation like a vessel. To do that, she removed her fingers from her knees and performed gentle conducting motions with them. Gerhard loved it when she directed and guided him in this intricate way, and adapted his words to the rhythm of her fingers. He tilted his head back slightly and took the last drag.

She wanted to know in precise detail what the desk had looked like and what had been lying on it. The request was accompanied by her forefinger and middle finger strolling gracefully through the air. Whether the room was stuffy or cool. How they had greeted each other. Now her middle fingers were moving in circles.

'What was hanging on the wall?' Gerhard had to improvise his answers to all these questions, which appeared within him like little bubbles and burst with a silent giggle before—with relative accuracy—he addressed them. He did still remember a few of

Blumenberg's deliberations, the professor's intense gaze, the relaxed way he sat in his armchair, his generous gestures, and also that he stood up, went to the wall unit and took a little Suhrkamp volume on the Nemean lion out of a drawer, then gave it to him; but little more than that. For Isa, Gerhard placed him behind his desk and invented towers of books on the desk, as well as a little aisle through which Blumenerg peered, as cunning as a mouse and nibbling on a roll. The air in the room had been more fresh than stuffy; his nose was reliable.

'And on the wall?' Isa was now sitting cross-legged, her hands placed on her knees like flat bowls.

'On the wall, yes, on the wall'—at first Gerhard wanted to say, 'an incredibly long wall unit and nothing else,' but then he found it too bland—'On the wall there was a poster of a painting by Patinir, the fugitive Holy Family sitting in the grass with little white sacks and a basket, taking a rest. Behind them a fantastically beautiful mountain landscape, with winding paths leading directly upwards into the blue.'

He was now as convinced by this Patinir as if he himself had just returned from a mountain hike in the holy region and handed his girlfriend a loaf of unleavened bread from one of the pouches.

'I was lucky this time,' Gerhard stated, 'the professor generously refrained from eating me once he had finished his roll.'

Isa laughed, but then slumped down. She herself would never have dared simply to barge into Blumenberg's office; she would already drop dead at the door, or at least be unable to utter a single word, or turn red as a lobster, or merely stammer. Gerhard corrected her: he had not simply walked through the door, but had made the appointment in writing beforehand, and everything after that went like clockwork. The professor was less difficult than everyone thought. One simply had to know what one wanted from him—as precisely as possible.

'But that's just it,' Isa said pensively, 'if one only knew what it was.'

Then there was supper in the communal kitchen. What was left of the joint's effect was dispelled in a heartbeat. Unsalted, overcooked spaghetti floated in watery tomato sauce; Biggi had done the cooking. Biggi was the pale and grumpy one with worry lines on her forehead, who never stopped chattering, talking down everything that went on in Münster, in America and in Germany, and constantly lecturing Isa, all the while looking askance at him. Philosophy was long obsolete, philosophical systems were edifices created by men to keep women intellectually in check, as much use as a hole in the head. (Biggi was studying education.) Facts ruled the world. The difference between men's and women's wage levels—a fact! Girls being disadvantaged by the education system—a fact! And, of course, most men were rapists, whether they admitted it or not. A double fact. She looked Gerhard in the eyes belligerently while saying this, but quickly returned her concentration to Isa to protect her from this rapist—though he seemed to have lost his grit at the moment, as crumpled as he was sitting at the kitchen table. All her concerns seemed focused on Isa, who inexplicably put up with it.

Though Isa was hardly grateful for these concerns. Enclosed in an invisible bubble, she picked apart some bread with her left hand and pushed tiny pieces of it in her mouth. The crumbs that lay scattered around her plate would have been enough to satisfy a twittering battalion of sparrows. She had not even been listening, but resurfaced from the bubble world she had slipped into with half-closed eyelids, bringing with her a few of her adventurous statements that overturned Biggi's concept, albeit not for long: 'Who said we were all made for each other?' (There was momentary confusion as to who had supposedly made such a claim.) 'It's no good if we just carry on as before.' 'We have to overcome all final pre-scriptions—after all, we are just preliminary forms of what we are meant to become.' 'One must do away with the absolutism of reality and become a figure of beautiful resignation.'

She raised a solitary noodle aloft with her fork and regarded it pensively.

Suddenly she began to giggle: 'Feminism is eating men whole, a crying shame, sooner or later nothing will be left of all the little swarming men.' Then her tone became conspiratorial: 'We must be very, very careful that the last man doesn't jump ship too,' and then she suddenly switched back to a cheerful tone: 'Perhaps the only ones left then will be the philosophers, but their interest in women is only so-so.'

Gerhard felt more uncomfortable than he had in a long time; he did not have the slightest desire for discussion, be it with a sociological autist or one à la Blumenberg. A stodgy calm spread through him. His face expressed clear doubts. He turned his head away, looked at the less-than-clean floor and fed Biggi's tomcat with a drop of tomato sauce he had dribbled onto his finger with a spoon. Objecting would have cost too much energy and fallen on deaf ears. He enjoyed the feeling of the cat's rough tongue on his finger. To take the deadlocked conversation in a different direction, he turned his head back towards the others and suggested somewhat tepidly that he cook some tasty roast beef with *spätzle* for everyone next week, whereupon Isa applauded with her finger tips.

Indeed, even Rena welcomed the idea. Rena was different from Biggi, more the independent type, taciturn. She was slightly podgy, with a pretty face and curly dark hair. Gerhard was bothered by the smell surrounding her. Rena smelt of sweat, which he found so repulsive that he stayed at a maximum distance. He regretted his suggestion with the roast beef the moment he made it. What an absurd idea to cook for people who got on his nerves so intensely (except for Isa, of course).

But the real surprise of the evening came when Isa was called to the telephone in the hallway and Rena disappeared in her room. Biggi sat down next to him and took her cat on her lap; it immediately switched on its purring. Biggi's hand wandered hesitantly over to Gerhard's, a handsome hand with long brown fingers, adorned by a signet ring and resting calmly on the wooden table, and it looked as if her slender white hand wanted to stroke his fingers; but she paused just before reaching it. Meanwhile the chubby-cheeked tomcat stared unwaveringly at the crawling fingers, as if waiting for the right moment to pounce with a swipe of its paw.

She said that she knew he was a nice chap who could be relied on. She was sorry for talking nonsense all evening. She was angry at another man, and everything got muddled up in her head. Nothing important. The only important thing was that they all had to look after Isa together. She had seen at once that he had a good influence on her, in fact a very good one. Now they all had to stick together and aim for the best.

Gerhard was caught off guard by this turn of events; he blushed with embarrassment, and could utter little more than a mumbled promise in reply. What surprised him most was Biggi's face: all hint of tenseness and surliness had vanished during this little confidential address. When Isa returned, the tom leapt down from Biggi's lap and stalked stiff-legged out of the kitchen.

Although things had perhaps taken a turn for the better, it was wiser not to call. The front door fell shut behind him with a metallic bang, as if it meant to lock him out for good. It was warm outside. He did not feel like turning back again and getting the bike from the cellar, so he went towards the city centre to read a news-paper and have a coffee.

As he crossed the Prinzipalmarkt, someone came cycling along. An apparition. All in white, in a flapping garment that could easily become entangled in the spokes, she entered the marketplace with head held high. He had not recognized her at first glance because she hardly ever wore white, if anything, a white T-shirt or white men's shirt. He waved his arms to stop her, and she actually braked.

'Where are you going?'

Her face was red. She gave him an unnecessarily long, pitying look before saying, in a highly inflated tone, 'To the field of honour.'

Pause.

She eyed him as if he had been up to no good. He was simply too limited to understand any of the essential things that flowed through her.

'Shall we go to a cafe and have a drink together?' he asked dispiritedly, for it was hardly likely that she would abandon intention, whatever it might be.

Isa lowered her head and frowned like a researcher with a tough nut to crack.

'That is an altogether absurd idea,' she whispered, 'absurd and inappropriate.'

'Why absurd?'

'For reasons,' she said sternly. 'I have to go.' There-upon she raised her head, looked at him radiantly and appended a sentence that seemed vaguely familiar from the last lecture: 'Relieved of all primal concern, into a friend-peopled sleep.'

Thus she spoke, and started pedalling again.

He was alarmed and stood there as if bewitched; he knew of no way to stop her, as she was already too far away to catch up on foot. There were no taxis he could have hailed in the deserted city to drive after her. He ran towards what looked from a distance like the sign for a taxi rank, but after reaching it he found it to be an advertising panel for Löwenbräu beer.

All-Encompassing Concern

There was no other way to dispose of the duty than to do it. For the sake of an old friend whose request to see him one last time he had been unable to refuse, he had to go to Isenhagen. It was a Sunday, and the weather was still fine when he left around lunchtime. On the way he cursed being kept from work. He had not subjected himself to such a long drive in years; the adventure would cost him hours. He would have thought that this friend in particular, who was now confronted with the phenomenon of lack of time with the utmost urgency, would have understood Blumenberg's ongoing struggle against his own lack of time and taken it into consideration. Had he, the friend, been robbed of so many years in his youth? Had he, the friend, ever found himself in a hopeless race to catch up with the stolen time and bring it into a demanding scholarly life, under the constant strain of pretending those stolen years had never existed? Evidently people still persisted in stealing his time.

After driving for a while along Amtsweg, at the forest's edge in Hankensbüttel, he reached an area with fairly small houses surrounded by gardens, but could not find Kurze Strasse. It had to be somewhere here. Blumenberg parked the car, got out and looked around for someone to ask.

Evidently there was no one around these parts in the late afternoon. Not even cyclists or summer visitors. Not a soul to be seen in the gardens. But no: over there, quite far away, there was a little black figure on the pavement. As he approached, Blumenberg wondered who this solitary figure might be, until he saw that he was walking towards a nun, a nun in a black habit and white coif busying herself with some bushes or other. Probably one of the conventuals from Isenhagen Abbey, Blumenberg thought.

She did not notice him approaching, preoccupied as she was, working away with garden shears, held clasped in white-gloved fingers, at a shrub whose richly blossoming branches hung over the fence; with the other hand, she held the branch that was to be cut and threw it to the ground with a gesture of displeasure.

'Excuse me,' said Blumenberg in the politest and most delicate way he could, 'might I ask you something?'

The little person turned around with a jolt; pointing the garden shears towards him combatively, she flashed her black eyes at him.

'Could you perhaps tell me where I can find Kurze Strasse?' Blumenberg asked.

The nun pointed wordlessly to the path along which he had come and abruptly twisted her head, which he took to mean that he should take the next right.

A peculiar attraction emanated from the nun. As small as she was (she barely came up to his shoulders) and as old as she might be (certainly ninety years or more)— Blumenberg had never seen such a concentration of energy in a person.

'Might I ask what you are doing there?' he heard himself say, and was surprised to have asked a question at all that might lead to complicated explanations at all; he glanced at the cut branches at their feet, then looked her in the eyes again.

The nun had a wonderful aged head, a flint-sharp tongue and a very light skin; her face was framed by an intricately pleated white lace coif, and under it there was a lace collar, also white. She was—he could not think of any better words for it—a *splendid, glorious figure*.

'As I see,' Blumenberg said, 'you are occupied with some extremely important business from which I shall not keep you any longer.'

'Right you are,' said the nun.

As he was just about to turn and leave with a word of farewell, she asked, 'Who is that with you?'

Blumenberg turned around in surprise, and indeed: the lion had accompanied him, creeping along behind him unnoticed.

'It's been following me for two days,' said Blumenberg, 'but normally no one notices it.'

'So!' The nun uttered the 's' with unusual sharpness. 'Then it is a mark of distinction!'

'Perhaps. Unfortunately I am not quite as sure as you seem to be. But tell me, now that we have made each other's acquaintance through my companion in a not entirely conventional way: what are you doing here? I don't doubt that you have serious business to tend to— my name, by the way, is Blumenberg.'

He extended his hand, which she hesitantly shook. She had now stopped pointing the shears at him and lowered them.

'Käthe Mehliss.'

The sharply hissed 's' lingered in his ear a little longer after the sound had faded. Once the conventual had told him her name, she immediately continued: 'Uncontrolled growth must be curbed. Where would we be if the pavements were overgrown too?'

As if to prove that the little conversation had by no means rendered her work obsolete, she seized another branch, cut it off and threw it at Blumenberg's feet.

'I can see at once that you are a perfectionist,' Blumenberg said appreciatively. 'You can't help it. You do it out of concern, the all-encompassing concern.'

'Creating order, maintaining order. Holding back uncontrolled growth. That is my duty. Wherever one looks, an unfathomable negligence rules. And that goes far beyond the plants.'

At the word 'duty', the tiny Mehliss stood bolt upright like a soldier: 'You are the first person to understand what I am doing. Not surprising, for you have it at your side.'

As if sensing encouragement from the nun, the lion looked up along her with interest, thought not very far up, for she was only slightly taller. It quietly accepted the fact that another branch had landed directly in front of its paws.

'You have earned it,' Käthe Mehliss said resolutely, 'Indeed, earned it.' With her black button eyes, she fixed her gaze on him more mildly than before.

'I presume you belong to the chapter of nuns at Isen-hagen,' said Blumenberg, and received a short 'Yes' in reply.

Käthe Mehliss only seemed to be interested in the lion now, and bent slightly down towards it. 'It has seen better days. You won't have very much time with it.'

She resumed her soldierly posture and looked Blumenberg sternly in the eye. 'Had you encountered it in its youth, you would have cowered before it. But now— oh well. Its days on earth are numbered; mine certainly are, and I daresay yours are too.'

Blumenberg could not stop marvelling. Perhaps the nun, with her amazing clear-sightedness, could also look back a little? Perhaps she knew whom the lion had accompanied before appearing in his study?

Käthe Mehliss smiled and declined—she was not authorized to divulge such information. She sent a quick glance upwards and added that a creature made for the glory of God was at home everywhere. He would have to ask for details elsewhere. And in any case, he was keeping her from her affairs.

Blumenberg bowed slightly. 'Goodbye,' he said. 'It was an honour to meet you, truly an honour.' With those words, he turned and went back the way he had come, accompanied by the lion.

Blumenberg finally found his friend's house, then found his friend with his wife around the back in the garden, sitting in a wicker chair under a copper beech. But before, when he had opened the latch on the garden gate, a Rottweiler had come bolting out and grimly confronted him. Blumenberg avoided meeting its gaze but spoke to it, and after a few sentences the dog relaxed—still scowling, as if it needed a moment to digest the fact that an important philosopher was speaking to it, and that it had been mistaken about this intruder. Then it became more trusting and led the visitor around the house and into the garden without any growling.

The delicately red spring leaves shimmered in the sunlight, a gently rocking sea of foliage, worthy of a poet's description. At first glance it was an idyll. Nonetheless, Blumenberg was determined to make the visit as short as possible. He found it hard to bear his friend's trembling, age spot-covered hands, his gurgling speech, the white gobs of saliva that had formed at the corners of his mouth, and his sentences—which now of all times, now that he had such difficulty uttering them, degenerated into blathering, accompanied by the impatience and displeasure with which he kept trying to drive away his wife, who busily brought everything for the coffee. Blumenberg found these scenes tormenting. He said nothing.

The lion did not appear.

Meanwhile, the spring freshness and clear sky he had enjoyed that morning had faded away imperceptibly. Driven along by warm air, clouds inserted themselves under the blue. The sky cloaked itself in a mouse-coloured grey, and only occasionally did a lone sunbeam break through the cover. The colours all around lost their radiance and became sleepy. Though they were sitting in the shady garden, Blumenberg felt the sweat beginning to break out on the back of his neck. He found it unpleasant. As far as bodily irritations were concerned, the gruesome sight of his friend was enough for him.

He kept thinking of the sharp-contoured face of Käthe Mehliss, which bore the signs of age in such glorious fashion. Her coif, which kept her head carefully wrapped like a jewel. The starkness and determination with which she chose her words. None of that in his friend. Only the terrible marks of flabby dissolution and decay. Yet he had once been a toned and muscular man, active and vigorous, who never felt himself above doing anything, a bundle of energy who had planned their joint trip to Egypt decades ago point by point in advance, then carried out the plan with remarkable tenacity. After three quarters of an hour, Blumenberg said goodbye to the ruin that had once been his friend and drove off, as if in a panic.

His fast pace was halted shortly before Münster. He found himself in a traffic jam and felt his anger mounting inside him. Why did he have to endure this idiotic delay as well? He banged furiously on the steering wheel, which did nothing to hasten his progress. When the flow of traffic stopped entirely, he got out, after waiting nervously for a few minutes, to survey the malaise. Far ahead, by a bridge, he saw blue lights flashing; evidently an accident. He turned his head to get an idea of the jam building up behind him and saw the lion reclining on the back seat. It was really far too cramped for the animal back there, and the whole car looked as if it was stuffed with lots of yellow fur. As if a switch had been flipped inside him, Blumenberg was calmed by the sight of the squashed-in lion, and his mood changed from impatience and anger to cheerfulness. He opened the rear door to give his lion a little relief.

In the meantime, the illumination of the sky had changed from a light, compact grey to a blackish, threatening darkness. Bulging clouds loomed, and a quick chase of fragments that had been torn away flew over them. To the left of the motorway, the forest extended up a hill in broad, dense black waves. Flashes of lightning twitched over him, running up and down. But the thunder was still quite far away.

The man in front of Blumenberg, a fat BMW driver whose buttons were virtually bursting off his striped shirt, which was hanging out over his trousers, had also got out of his car. Very carefully, like some precious treasure, he held a tiny wire-haired dachshund pressed against his chest, then put it on the ground and attached a pink leash to its pink collar. The little dog had kept quiet at the man's chest, but as soon as it felt the asphalt under its crooked legs it floundered this way and that, as far as the short leash allowed. When it looked in the lion's direction by chance it froze for a moment, but then continued scurrying around as before.

Blumenberg laughed to himself and became involved in a conversation with the man about the wilful character of dachshunds, which one was powerless to change (though little Maxl was a laudable exception); they spoke, the one with Lübeckish sharpness and the other with the Franconian rolled 'r', about the merits of wire-haired over short-haired dachshunds, made predictions about the weather brewing above their heads, and how long this nuisance would last—here Blumenberg, one arm draped casually across the roof of his Peugeot and drumming fast-paced syncopations on the roof with his fingertips, identified himself as an optimist (in which he proved right), while the BMW driver was a die-hard pessimist.

Thick drops began to fall, bursting loudly on the car roof. Blumenberg quickly shut the rear door and got back in the front. Stuffing the lion back onto the narrow seat required no effort whatsoever, as he felt no pressure against the car door.

Slowly, halting again and again, the convoy began to move. Blumenberg drove slightly more quickly past the site of the incident, with blue lights flickering around it, where a yellow truck stood behind the motorway bridge in the right lane. By now it was pouring, and the windscreen wipers were working at full steam. It was impossible to tell what kind of accident had occurred; at least, there was no damaged car at the side.

No. 255431800

Isa dressed herself in white around three in the afternoon. A long, flowing crepe dress, white stockings, and some girlish strap shoes made of punched leather that she had bought years ago and never worn. She stood in front of the mirror in those clothes and felt ridiculous. Like a debutante with a white pearl necklace, certainly not like Patti Smith. All she needed was the wreath of field flowers in her hair and a solstice smile. She wrinkled her mouth. 'Like an ironic flourish, this mouth,' she told herself, but was simultaneously enraptured by her own image. Her eyes so deep, deep, deep. The skin so white. Everything so white. The eyebrows like brackets laid flat—now raised, now lowered, raised again and lowered again, wasn't that pretty? Was she not a wonder machine? The wonder machine had previously been forced to lead a soul-destroyingly insipid life—no, not soul-destroying, but rather gliding along stagnantly in an eternal half-sleep; why so stagnant, could anyone tell her why? But it had disintegrated behind her, this stagnant, insipid life. And what was coming now? Something great, pale, willing; she picked up a paper parasol that had been stuck to a piece of cocktail melon and opened it, closed it, opened it.

'Benedictus,' she breathed, 'putting right the all-pervasive lack of reliability in the world, that's the point, isn't it? Benedictus,' she breathed in the direction of the mirror, as if invoking someone from thin air, and began to hum to herself.

It was pouring with rain.

Suddenly she drew her eyebrows together, raised her finger reprovingly and said with deadly seriousness: 'Last time the words gushed out of you rather shame-lessly, like slime, but I heard them, yes indeed, I heard and understood.'

She went to the shelf, rewound the music cassette, pressed 'play' and dreamily said 'Goodness gracious,' as if the device were new to her.

The River now sounded for the twenty-second time—loudly, far more loudly than usual. No one complained. Her housemates had gone out, and the tomcat had snuck away. Springsteen was going on a water trip, ' . . . *down to the river*'; he savoured the 'down' with ardour, roaring about the impoverished and ill-fated young couple; down-stream, downwards, ever further down into the churning water, the journey of love, an insistent suction, and poured out of the open windows—smooth, powerful and dark. Naturally Blumenberg was not a builder working for the Johnstown Company; his construction work took place on paper. But Blumenberg's burning gaze came alive through Springsteen's voice, and his eyes stared at her.

It was pouring with rain.

She looked at one of her buttons as if she had never seen it before. It was small and white, with teeth like a gearwheel; there was a black line going around it once under the teeth. It was not one from her father's factory; such buttons were not manufactured there. She thought of the polishing drums standing in a line at the front of the factory, filled with bits of wood and polishing paste, in which shimmering mother of pearl buttons were turned until they shone.

She had cut the buttons off an old flea market blouse and sewn them to her dress. A long time ago she had heard a radio play from the 1950s in which girls disappeared and buttons were made from them. Beautiful buttons, unique buttons, at least as beautiful as the one she was holding in her fingers, pulling up the thin fabric like a pointy little mountain. Perhaps she was wearing lots of button-girls over her bosom? How many were there? One, two, three, four, five—six. Maybe she was a button-girl too, but still had her transformation ahead of her.

She let go of the button and paced back and forth in front of the windows. Maybe she should drive past his house, just to see if the bouquet was still in front of the entrance.

She was sure it wouldn't be.

The Alfa had refused to start when she wanted to go to the cinema last night, and would undoubtedly remain equally motionless now. Twenty-four white lilies, wrapped in white silk paper, a green velvet ribbon wound around it with a tiny card—the sort of velvet ribbon worn on dresses in the Rococo period to tie up the bosom. Inside the wrapping at the bottom, a little sachet of *Blumenfrisch* to keep them fresh for longer. This annoyed her; the sachet was the height of silliness. How long did flowers keep at most, even if regularly watered and pruned? Five days, ten days? She did not know, having no experience with cut flowers. She would not be surprised if he hated flowers.

Springsteen was now roaring down the dried-up riverbed for the twenty-third time.

The card! Had he even read it? Surprised? Amused? Turned the thing around between his fingers and said something clever or slimy about it? Or had his wife found the bouquet and thrown it in the rubbish at once along with the card? What had possessed her to do something so ridiculous! If he had read it, that made it doubly, triply embarrassing. Embarrassing, embarrassing, embarrassing. Now she did not want to remember what she had written. Blah, blah, blah—the typical infatuated hogwash—*because I cannot help adoring you with every fibre of my heart*. What idiocy! Adoring a man with a bald pate and a little wavy fringe of hair at the sides. Pure idiocy. She had only been pulling his leg. She had not revealed her name but he was sure to know; he had kept looking at her during the lecture, he had glanced up, looked at her and ignited the great light in her eyes. Yes, yes, the great light. Since then she had been blessed—no, what nonsense, tormented in his name.

(Isa could not know that the situation with the bouquet had taken an entirely different turn from what she
imagined and feared. A young man walking past No. 30
Grüner Weg at dusk had seen the bouquet lying behind
the garden gate, slipped inside unnoticed and stolen it to
give to his beloved; naturally he tore off the card and
threw it in a bin, where it went through the usual process
of emptying, transportation and finally incineration.)

Her skin tingled with confusion. He and she lived in
a petty world full of 'no'. She would now unfold all that
was in her: everything bad, good, stupid, clever, embarrassing. Time to begin with her own inner interpretation
of the world. Embarrassing, she was embarrassing. She
had failed to secure the irrevocable favour of her god and
had thus become embarrassing.

It was pouring with rain. She was soaked.

'Shit!' she yelled, drowning out Springsteen.

They were not two desperate young folks, not Romeo
and Juliet from provincial America with no way out.
Embarrassing, embarrassing: the god of her choice was
an old man.

It was pouring with rain. The windscreen wipers swung
like crazy. Blumenberg opened the car door.

With Springsteen's voice in her head and a little bag
slung over her shoulder, Isa wandered out of the room,
wandered out of the apartment, not wasting the effort to
shut the door behind her, wandered to her bicycle, which
she had left in front of the house unlocked, mounted the

saddle and set off. It was only after cycling a hundred metres or more that Springsteen's voice became inaudible.

It was fun to ride about in the empty streets on a warm afternoon. How stupid that Gerhard of all people had to cross her path in the middle of town, but maybe not so stupid; he was entitled to a meaningful utterance that would always stay with him. But she could not let herself be distracted, least of all by him—Gerhard was stubborn, not one to give up so easily. She cycled off again and cycled and cycled, and it was a miracle that the long flapping dress did not get caught in the spokes; she knew the way, which she had often driven in her Alfa, it led out of town along wide roads where the traffic greatly increased and she herself, she could feel it very clearly, was seen in her white dress as an angel, a flower girl from nowhere who did not belong in such traffic, in the middle of all the Sunday day trippers who overtook her bemusedly, nothing, absolutely nothing could happen to her, she could even have ridden into the oncoming traffic, she was the living antithesis of the world and on the run, to flee is also to act, and Blumenberg—Blumenberg had imposed this antithesis on her, Blumenberg had made her realize, he was driving her along from behind with his long, incredibly long forefinger, which he had pushed into her back, penetrating her heart: 'Ride, ride, ride on, my poor little soaked soul, ride, beating your wings and growing hot in your white dress, bridal in your awareness in the manner of angels, not humans.'

The sky had lost its lightweight blue and covered itself in lead. Isa was sweating. Her fingers clenched the handlebars.

Having reached her destination, she awkwardly dismounted from the bicycle. On a bridge with cars driving through nose to tail underneath it, three lanes going out and three lanes coming back. Every movement counted now, no matter how small, although her arms and legs, covered with a film of sweat, shaky and crampy from the long ride, were not obeying properly. A flock of squawking birds flew towards the distant forest. There was coarse mockery in their voices. Don't be deterred. The movements had to be carried out in full; a guru had commanded her to raise and lower her legs, raise and lower her arms, stand and walk slowly, roll over from heel to toes, rock back and forth on tiptoe, and keep going.

She had put the pearl handbag in the bicycle basket. A present from her mother. This was quite a special handbag, for a prisoner had sewn pearl after pearl onto it, a mildly kitschy product of patience that she had always kept in her cupboard, for she could not possibly walk about in Münster with a pearl handbag on a chain, such a dainty, sweet little thing taken to evenings at the theatre or the opera by women with permed hair. But because a prisoner had made it—a lifer, no less—she cherished the purse all the same.

'My gender bag,' she said aloud, and it conjured a smile on her face—it even had a red inner lining.

What exactly was in the gender bag? Hmm? A mild wind blew through her thin hair. She pondered with knotted eyebrows like a child that has to add five and seven, while her hands clasped the bridge's railing and her right leg swung over to the other side: a hundred-mark note, stupid, you should know that, in the little purse with the button that doesn't close properly, a bit of small change, most likely a five-mark coin and a few tenners, and what about the tissue, hmm? What do you need a tissue for? One or two tissues, crumpled up, full of snot, hmm? Not folded nicely, not clean—and oh, what do we have in the tiny little inside pocket? A Chanel lipstick, bright red, that gives a dry click when one takes of the lid, and the powder compact, the little tinny-tin-tin, another dainty thing with fake diamonds as star inlays on a blue background, when you open it the eyes flash open like a charmer, the innocent thing. So what else? Something more and something else, we'll never be finished at this rate: the eyebrow pencil whose lid always slides down, a lipliner—down in the traffic a big, long, yellow lorry appeared—and don't forget, yes, don't forget, what? The ID card of course, you little idiot, what's the matter with you, a good Swabian girl always has her ID with her, issued in Heilbronn with a picture where the little person in black and white looks as if she were angry at the world, but what in God's name, what's that sparrow up to on the railing, twitching its head in such a funny way, and—now the left leg had swung over, her hands had let go, and she was already flying too, flying like an angel—

People say that life passes by in a flash during one's final seconds, but that was not the case here. Isa thought of her eyebrow pencil. Not of Blumenberg, as one would have expected. No doubt the lid had come off again and the pencil had smeared up the inner lining; she flew, thinking with all her might of the smears, and clenching her teeth so hard that it splintered off the left upper incisor. But that was negligible compared to everything that splintered and broke when the body hit the asphalt.

A Brief Interlude about Where the Narrator's Responsibility Ends

What does a narrator know and what do they not? It is questionable whether a narrator can really know the last thoughts to enter the mind of a suicide. Naturally the narrator has noted down in minute detail what clothes were worn, the nature of the legacy, how the dead body looked, and how people close by and further away reacted to it; all they need to do is choose artfully, omit artfully and must not try overly hard to turn on the little counting machine (otherwise, the result would be someone dying unnoticed and with no emotional attachment under a huge pile of trivialities). Assuming all this is taken into account, and then lo and behold, a life in letters snuffs itself out before the eyes of the empathetic reader.

A suicide like that acts conclusively, even if they hesitated a little beforehand, or some bit of fidgeting or other holds them up—which the narrator knows, of course, having been able to observe them for days, weeks or perhaps months preparing the whole mess. But what exactly the suicide was thinking? Racing thoughts, frozen thoughts in their last moments? Or a complete retrospective, viewed in slow motion on the inside and fast motion from the outside? A second of the egg being fertilized? The scream at birth, the first smack on the bottom? Do those things not preserved by the puny memory return with a vengeance? Beyond the individual memory? Passing through all forms taken on earth to the nanosecond of creation, so that everything one has ever been is imaginatively destroyed within a second, and the great consumption takes away every entry ever made in all of existence?

In however superior a fashion the narrator might claim to be in the know, they are merely fishing air out of the air in this case. If they were honest, they would have to pass. The case of Isa seems clear at first. We are dealing with an infatuated woman who has become trapped in the irrealis. A giant cloud of erotic longing carries this delicate person around, swollen with unfulfillable wishes reaching up to heaven; at their tyrannical command she jumps off the bridge. This is all plausible so far. Darkening propels and inflates individuals, coating them in false sugar, until enjoyment is no longer possible within reality. But does reality not claw doggedly at the moribund soul at the moment when it is too late? When a circumspect return is no longer possible? And in what form does the real flash up and shine with fantastic radiance? At the tiny level, as the content of a bag with odds and ends? Or differently, as a sparrow whose abrupt hop and turn of the head hold such cheerfulness and elegance that one should really just run through one's hands through one's hair and chuckle with mirth? (The irony of the sparrow: if Isa had touched her hair, she would have lost her balance and gravity would have done her in too.)

At any rate, the narrator is highly attached to the idea that the suicide is mocked at the last moment by the reality they have so rejected and neglected. As if all the fake magic had been blown away. 'If truth then comes running along stark naked' to quote Brentano, everything is reversed. It is strong and substantial, the truth of life. It laughs at the suicide and makes a pitiful idiot of them. (The narrator would not, of course, apply this theory to people who kill themselves to escape torture or extermination, or those for whom the body is no longer anything but a source of pain. Nor had the narrator ever ridiculed the scene in which Socrates drained the cup of poison. But Socrates was Socrates, an old man dried up with dignity who realistically assessed what awaited him.)

Naturally the reader is free to think what they like. In the case of Isa, they might believe that she leapt towards the phantom of Blumenberg and not a single snippet of reality managed to insert itself between them. Let them do so; the reader cannot be contradicted.

As the narrator themselves has been introduced here, they will be allowed to intervene equally impudently in a further matter before disappearing from this tale for good:

Gerhard. Gerhard, whom we have all become fond of, and whom we surely wish a long life. The narrator, once again the sovereign ruler over time and also a little bit the fact-pusher we already know, now reaches for a grappling hook and hauls in a later hour. To be precise: the hour that struck fifteen years, seven months and four days after that fatal Sunday in May.

Back then, of course, in 1982, Gerhard could not know that he was one of only a few of Blumenberg's students who would make successful progress in academia, advancing comfortably without any great excitement or obstacles. Baur simply carried on as before, made few enemies and was respected, or at least liked, wherever he went. Little did he know, thank God, that the fate of his prematurely departed parents was ticking away as a speeding clock inside him, an evil time clock that would put an abrupt end to his promising career.

When, in 1997, just under a year after the death of his teacher—Baur was now thirty-nine years old, and had a prestigious habilitation to his name—he applied for a professorship in the philosophy department of the ETH Zurich, auditioning so breathtakingly that he ended the race as the champion horse. Directly after the lecture, much of which had been devoted to his old favourite hero Samson, and for which he received effusive congratulations from his normally reserved Swiss hosts, he suddenly bent double in the corridor of the ETH, collapsed, and died a few hours later at the university hospital as a result of a stroke. Baur left a wife, an eight-year-old daughter, a boy of one and a half, and an extremely cheerful, not yet fully-housetrained terrier he had given his children for Christmas.

But enough of the obituaries. Let us now shoo the narrator back whence they came.

Egypt

He had returned to Altenberge after his strenuous Sunday outing. The ruffled stormy sky had calmed itself, the rain had stopped, but so much water had plummeted from the sky that the trees stood in the darkness heavy with moisture, black masses that constantly dripped and had gurgling sounds coming from their feet. Large puddles had formed along the way to the house and were difficult to avoid. He swore it would be the last such excursion, took off his wet shoes, washed his hands and rinsed his face with cold water. He was not in the mood for supper and not in the mood for speaking. He wanted to dry off and find himself again.

A sand-coloured cashmere pullover that he usually wore in his study, comfortably cut like a sports shirt with a collar, was conducive to calm. He had several of them in different colours. When he lay down on the sofa in the music room, warmed by the familiar homely wool, his thoughts gradually returned to shallower waters.

The night wrapped itself around him again, thank God. Blumenberg felt the protection of the night with rare intensity. It released him from his gloominess and duty to be sociable. Spared him foolish surprises and loosened up his intellectual apparatus. He had taken a record out of its cover with fine, circumspect fingers, wiped over it with a cloth and placed it on the turntable. Blumenberg loved the moment when the tone arm descended and the stylus gently made contact with a groove. It crackled. He quickly made for the sofa so that he would already be lying down when the first notes sounded. One of his favourites was playing. Arturo Benedetti Michelangeli played the Schubert sonata as if raising each finger for a fraction of a second after touching the key—a sign admonishing the listener to pay very close attention to the note already fading; even when the music found itself murmuring in swampy depths, even when it rang up and down in cascades, winding its pearl garlands and dallying a little, one could still hear the individual notes quite clearly, especially the bright ones, which the pianist sometimes pushed almost to the point of pain. Blumenberg kept his eyes closed. The twitching in Benedetti Michelangeli's monkish face, which he had once seen on TV, was present again, along with his statement that every actual note was still infinitely far from what was possible, and it was painful to have to content oneself with this inadequacy. This way of playing was not for romantic revellers whose hearts longed to be carried off in a roaring storm; Benedetti Michelangeli played for people like him, who derived secret pleasure from analysis, the structural fibres of the music, the precision of its reproduction—people who preferred to sense for themselves the subtle emotional qualities behind the musician's dutiful zeal for exactitude, rather than receiving heart commands from the pianist and being forced to submit to them.

He did not care whether the lion was lying on the rug in his study again. One even gets used to something as extraordinary as a lion, he thought contently, enjoying the way the pianist kept jolting him out of his mental undulations with his sharp high notes.

Naturally the lion's appearance was a miracle. Blumenberg was not one to sneer or poke fun at miracles; on the contrary, the demonstrative and affirmative power of the miracles that took place at the time the Old and New Testament were written, and still as late as early Christianity, impressed him with their intensity and referential power, even if he could not bring himself to believe in them. But the lion embodied the miracle. In addition, its existence had been confirmed in Isenhagen by a witness whose reliability was beyond all doubt. As soon as an inkling of doubt had stirred in him and threatened to harm today's encounter, the impressive head of the little Mehliss had shown itself and gazed at him with eyes as black as coal. What more did he want, damn it? Did he believe in miracles or not? Most of all: did he believe in the validity of the miracle he had experienced, which powerfully bound, nay, chained him—Blumenberg, the son of a Jewish mother, an agnostic baptized a Catholic, who, in his time of need when no university would accept him, had been allowed to study for a few semesters at the Jesuit College in Frankfurt, which had moved to Limburg, and who had never left the church—to the two Testaments? Whose aim, which he kept attempting to formulate in writing, was to prevent the conception of God found in them from breaking apart?

March '39. Wolfanger's face, twisted with repulsion. The director of the Katharineum, who had refused in public to shake his hand, the hand of the best pupil in all of Schleswig-Hostein.

Blumenberg got off the sofa with a jolt and turned over the record. He was no more willing to submit to the power of the miracle than he was to let the power of the music overcome him. Or to let the past consume him.

He refused to be ambushed by the miracle; he could perhaps have come to terms with a delicate announcement of the miraculous. To what end had he built a sublime intellectual enclosure and wrapped himself in it, to what end had he been granted a sharp mind and a deep-seated distrust of the states of arousal that led humans astray, to what end did he possess an outstanding memory—all this only to sit there like a child, fold his hands and gaze at his lion with shining eyes?

He thought of his friend, whose tailspin towards the end testified to his abandonment, even though his wife looked after him conscientiously. If nothing but the body remained and no salvation harboured the finite human being in the hollow of its hand, the body performed a terrible theatre, grasping greedily at every remaining scrap of life. How triumphant, how different it had been when they were both in full possession of their faculties and boldly undertaken, together with their wives, the great trip to Egypt for three radiant months in 1956. Blumenberg saw his friend's big Mercedes floating through the air on ropes. In Antwerp, that city scarred so heavily by the war, it was hoisted by a crane onto the *Arethusa*. From there they went on to Genoa, where they were loaded onto another freighter with everything they had, the night-blue Mercedes and an impressive number of suitcases, and finally arrived in Alexandria.

Already on the first leg of the voyage, on the Atlantic along the coasts of France and Spain, he felt a relief he had rarely known. He never tired of staring at the water, watching birds that accompanied the ship. He had never taken an extended journey on the sea, although he had always liked being in the water. As a boy he had been an excellent diver, able to stay underwater far longer than his friends; sometimes they already thought he had drowned, until he came shooting up in a flash of water before the anxious clique, gasping for air, and his friend Ulrich exclaimed, 'What! You're alive!'

The solitude of the diver became glorious as soon as the water covered him and the sounds of the world above had faded. Now his body remained dry, but he found himself dealing with an entirely different mass of water. He had embarked, had reached a free, unpredictable zone, gradually breaking away from the land, the coastline no more than a narrow strip, until it finally withdrew entirely, giving him an exhilarated feeling of courage. Geometry, the measure of the earth, had vanished. A smile of intelligence floating above the hazy grey-blue.

Other thoughts burst in unbidden. Zerbst. Blumenberg turned over on his left side and tried to concentrate on the music again.

The disappearance of the earth. He imagined what was missing to the rhythm of Benedetti Michelangeli's runs, simultaneously inverting the perspective and the emotional attachment—not he but the land, coasts and cities would suffer because he had distanced himself from them; to the same extent as they withdrew from him, they would now miss him. He was amused by the thought of who and what would suffer because of him, who was leaning against the railing in so leisurely a manner, enjoying the sight of the sea foam churned up by the boat's keel.

One time, in rough sea not far from the Spanish coast, a tousled albatross had strayed onto the upper deck. He could not help thinking of 'The Rime of the Ancient Mariner', Coleridge's verse tale of the shot-dead albatross that was so precious to the English. What would it be like to have the dead albatross laid around one's neck and watch all one's comrades die? The bird flew away, that is to say, it turned around and waddled along the wet wooden surface in a pitifully comical fashion before rising into the air and descending once more into the waves, on which it evidently bobbed up and down comfortably with its broad wings. Even this exhausted elderly bird had the power to lift the burden of the dead off him; in the salty air, it granted him a relief that lasted for the entire journey, deep into the hot Egyptian desert.

He had packed Thomas Mann's novel *Joseph and His Brothers*, and read it for the third time in his cabin at night with new eyes, amid the rocking waves, full of anticipation for Egypt.

In the sea, the formless was at home. The ancient philosophers had warned of the sea, which was ruled by the untameable Poseidon; they had warned of sin if humans ventured out into the unseemly and measureless, when they made connections with countries and peoples that had been separated by a wise providence. The Bible also knows this fundamental distrust towards the sea. But Blumenberg had not the slightest spark of scepticism: he loved the sea. And the little crowd of guests that had come together on the freighter—comprising, besides him, a Dutch couple, two Frenchmen, an English diplomat and a German businessman—loosened him up, giving him a feeling of freedom he had seldom experienced.

His high spirits continued during the gatherings in the captain's mess. He ate with relish, was splendidly tipsy, not seasick for a second, and became a valued entertainer for the guests, who had grown curious about the fiery young professor who blustered about with such acumen and wit.

He got on tremendously well with his friend. They spoke about music, about Benedetti Michelangeli's adventures as a pilot and racing driver, about the future of technology, about the enthusiasm and demonization with which it was met, which did little to impede its constant progress. They were both motoring buffs; they could talk shop about the performance of vehicles with the passion of children playing with car trump cards, even at sea where the Mercedes was not driving a metre, resting firmly tied-down in the ship's hold. His father's chauffeur had showed him at an early age how to drive a car. A Horch 670 twelve-cylinder. His passion for cars came from those childhood days. Now he was looking forward to taking turns with his friend navigating his Mercedes through an unknown land.

He knew Venice and Florence, but not Genoa. The city was a sensation beneath a clear blue sky, steeply ascending the mountain. Down below, viewed from the port, it was a magnificent specimen that had flourished through the trading skills of merchants and seemed to be bursting at the seams with pride, and contributed so much to the *grandezza* of Italian architecture.

By now the tone arm had returned to its resting position. Blumenberg had been so immersed in the memory of his Egyptian adventure that he had not even noticed the ending of the music.

Alexandria. Flatly built, with isolated skyscrapers still under construction, dazzlingly bright, a drawn-out coastal settlement, a jumble of people, shops, restaurants, large and small boats, and separated from those the battle fleet. They had landed in Egypt shortly before the outbreak of the Suez Crisis, in the months when it could get boiling hot in mainland Egypt, forty-five degrees and more. They had arrived in the land of Gamal Abdel Nasser. With a prominent nose and elegantly greying temples, the tall officer looked like an actor. The sly fox had only been in power for two years. He hated the Jews, and 'Pan-Arabism' was the magic word with which he rose to become the leader of the Arab world.

Hanging by ropes again, the Mercedes was placed gently on land, and the engine—being a work of technical precision that could be relied on—sprang to life as soon as his friend turned the ignition key and pressed the black Bakelite start button. The climatic changes to which the car had been exposed those last two weeks had not done any damage. Now it was shining in the Egyptian sun, ready to resume its duty.

Cairo surpassed everything that Blumenberg had imagined or learned from guidebooks. They stayed at the Mena House, in the old palace hotel in the middle of enormous gardens with a direct view of the pyramids. His heart leapt for joy when he entered his suite. The rooms were works of east-west magic: English luxury in the bathroom, the exquisite antiques, and the oriental latticework in front of the windows, where richly embroidered decorative cushions lay scattered on benches and divans.

He reached for his pillow, which had become deformed into a hard sausage under his head, and punched it back into shape.

The Mena House. The breakfast served there was English. The tea, imported from Fortnum & Mason in

London, was English. The waiters had been drilled in English fashion. The palm trees in richly decorated pots were oriental. Here he finally felt back in his element, as the son of an art and antiques dealer who, after the meagre postwar years, could once again enjoy a luxury that had surrounded him decades ago as a child, albeit in a different form. Viewed from the hotel, Cairo in the morning was cloaked in mist; the city exuded a pink-grey veil that lay on top of it like a cover, and the cover only lifted—if at all—around midday.

Driving the Mercedes from the hotel into Cairo proved to be an adventure. As soon as the memories of it went through his mind, Blumenberg's fingers were willing to clasp the steering wheel once again. Anyone who could move and anything that could be moved jostled about in the streets. Camel riders, nimble Topolinos, heavy Russian state carriages, donkey carts, horse-drawn carts, trucks with exhaust pipes that belched forth hellish black clouds, minibuses, flocks of sheep, porters with vendor's trays strapped on or sacks slung over their shoulders. It was a challenge to cruise carefully around everything that was moving there, all the while keeping an eye on the oncoming traffic, which was an equally chaotic affair.

Viewed up close, the poor and ordinary Cairo was also spectacular. Still at the hotel, they came under the care of an educated guide who spoke excellent English and of whom they quickly became fond, Hassan, who accompanied them through all the months. Blumenberg's friend had selected and hired this guide in advance through his worldwide business connections. Hassan was an extremely sharp young man from a wealthy family. Dressed in his white *jalabiya*, he led them right into the bustle of the city, a labyrinthine tangle in which every spot was used or occupied by traders, corner men and door-men waiting for a little job, by people who sat around and chatted or drove their sheep through the streets. A tanner was squatting in front of a tub, smoothing a ram's fleece. Desert camels swayed past stallholders. One was deco-rated as if going to its own wedding, with tassels and hangings; even flashing gold coins that had been woven into the browband. French-style city houses that could have lined a Parisian boulevard alternated with oriental buildings and their railings, which extended far over the streets. Between them stood new constructions in the Mediterranean Bauhaus style and huts that were virtually collapsing. The bars and cafes were stimulating. They were packed with young men in discussion and older water pipe smokers, and between them heavily made-up women in tight Western outfits.

Their wives had had desert clothes tailored especially for the trip to Egypt—colourful dresses they would never have worn in Germany, as well as comfortable shorts that ended just under the knees and blouses made of paper-thin cotton. On their heads they wore hats with particularly wide brims to shield them from the sun. Blumenberg's attire was more conventional. For walking about in the city he wore a thin, light-coloured linen suit with an elegant straw hat on his head.

He needed some time to get used to the compulsive chatter of the Egyptians. Wherever they walked or stood, they produced crowds simply to chatter loudly and wave their hands. At first it was too much for him. And the intrusive demands, 'Bakshish! Bakshish!', especially from the children, got on his nerves. Pulling on his jacket, holding out their hands. He endeavoured to keep people away from him. The tendency towards kitsch and opulence, and the heavy smell of perfume emanating from the upper-class women, in particular, were a source of discomfort.

But then something clicked. Their vitality had over-whelmed his resistance. He suddenly enjoyed watching them. And sometimes the after-effects of Mann's novel became disproportionately great, for example, when he found himself on the lookout for Potiphar's wife in the hotel receptionist, or some wife or other at the side of an affluent state official. Even on the sofa the enjoyment still continued, leading him to turn on his right side again. The Egyptians were born actors. They performed an opulent theatre of gestures for one another, their voices gliding high up and then coming down again. Their large-eyed, nose-centred faces exuded good-naturedness; their gestures, which often involved holding out their palms freely as in a display of generosity, made them appealing.

Thanks to Hassan, who quickly understood that he was not dealing with typical travellers who were only interested in pyramids and pharaohs' tombs, they ended up in the cinema, watching a film by Youssef Chahine, which became a subject of heated debate in the Greek club they subsequently visited. A black-and-white film in the style of Italian neo-realism with many amateur actors, all of whom were gifted comedians. The film was a small revelation, and could easily stand alongside the best films he had ever seen. Much of the plot evaded him, of course. All he remembered was that it began at a train station, and that a roguish, worldly-wise kiosk-owner suddenly found himself embroiled in extremely amusing situations.

Hassan led them through labyrinthine backyards to an old wooden Dervish theatre, a little circular building with spire lights, decorated with finely carved lattices on the inside to partition off the women from the men. An elderly guard was sitting in front of it amid a mass of kittens and told them cat stories, of which Hassan translated some fragments; the old man would point to each animal and imitate the way it meowed, hissed or toddled off proudly. How surprised he was by his friend, who showed no inhibitions in sitting down on the stone steps next to the guard and trying out a few sentences of broken Arabic on him. The old man responded with laughter, his mouth wide open, revealing only a few isolated teeth sticking out.

Matterhorn: the mere name was already an in-joke between them. Whenever it became so hot in front of pyramids that every movement was an effort, and they would have liked nothing more than to sink into bathtubs filled with cold water, they kept their spirits up with Matterhorn jokes. Standing in the blazing sun, they got in position as if posing for a group photo at the snowy summit, waving their arms as if to keep warm, shielding their eyes with their hands and looking around—just as if they were surrounded by high mountains, with an ice-cold wind blowing.

The Nile, again and again the Nile. Rightly sung and invoked. They travelled along the Nile on an old paddle steamer, and every evening there was a surprise awaiting them in their cabin. The steward looking after them skilfully arranged the pyjamas and nightshirts in such a way that they were welcomed to their beds by animal-like constructs: a swan, a snake or a crocodile. The steward received their praise with a mixture of embarrassment and pride, and their encouragement led him to attempt increasingly complex shapes.

One could see from the ship that the slim green strip along the river, the space into which all life and agricultural activity was squeezed, was very narrow. Water buffalo stood in the fields. Ibises stalked about. It was quite conceivable that crocodiles were lurking close to the riverbank. Behind the hills the sand dunes already began, a wide desert landscape, sparsely populated by nomads passing through, if at all. Time and again their ship was surrounded by cockleshells filled with frolicking children screaming and jumping into the water, waving like mad to the passengers.

The number of monuments they had visited! Fifty? A hundred? He could not even count them all. Naturally they had been in the Valley of the Kings and descended into the brightly coloured tombs; naturally they had visited the temples of Thebes and Karnak, and far south Abu Simbel, the rock palace, which at that time had not yet been moved to make space for the new dam and was still in its original place, as well as the temples on the island of Elephantine and many more. They had found the colossal statues at the entrances eerie—too forbidding, too large, too smooth. Yet in their totality they were sublime, a culture of death-defiance in the desert sands, with majestic headwear and beards. A culture that was difficult to relate to contemporary Egyptians, like those bustling about chaotically in Cairo. The Egypt of the past looked down disinterestedly at that of the present. Its efforts to escape the absolutism of reality had been immense; there was nothing comparable. Increasing the worth of one goal, namely to wrest life from death, by making its architectural consummation enormously difficult. Such immense existence-heightening feats could no longer be grasped by the country's modern-day inhabitants and foreign visitors. Fragments of lines by Edna St Vincent Millay floated through his mind—'The kings of Egypt; even as long ago . . . with long eye and scented limbs they slept, and feared no foe . . . Their will was law; their will was not to die: And so they had their way; or nearly so.'

He loved that 'or nearly so'. Forever—but not quite. The boats for the dead were perfect, nearly perfect with the outstretched wings above them. They remained etched in his memory more than almost anything else. How unique to reach the realm of the dead with the help of a barge—a narrative of great pictorial intensity, and a plausible wishful construct to boot. Poetry and terror floated above death; the escort of the barges moderated the terror into gentle importance.

And yet—he was seized more than once by the thought that it had been a mistake to travel to Egypt, into this grey-red wasteland that extended to the horizon. He should have turned back in Bruges. For ultimately, he liked to stay at home and preferred to bring the world into his chamber and envision it in radiant thought-images, rather than expose himself to the activity and lose himself helplessly in it, however exciting the things he saw may have been at first glance. In the long run it was a strain on him to be constantly in company, barely able to use even an hour purely for himself in a shielded environment.

The writing monkeys on the walls of the burial chambers were a frivolous sight, sitting on their backsides like tax collectors—a welcome change from the dominant severity of the ancient kingdoms. He had wandered past a thousand stern figures with legs turned sideways, displaying their tools or sitting in statuary fashion wearing tall headdresses and receiving something, the arms usually slightly raised in a showing gesture. In his heart, these figures remained alien to him. Only the busts of Akhenaten at the Cairo Museum, which were so conspicuously different, had magically drawn him. He saw the extremely stretched-out skull, the long nose and the elegantly curled mouth of the peculiar king in his mind. The giant museum was a curious place, a mix of pomp and broom cupboard. Piles of scarabs. Heaps of amulets. When one opened a door somewhere, bandaged mummies came falling out. And sitting above all the bustle and ruinous chaos, time and again, the oddly smiling king. His melancholy flair carried him further and further away.

And as he lost himself in his couch, he found himself sitting on the terrace of the Old Cataract Hotel in Aswan again, gazing at the Nile, gazing at the red-golden sky that poured flames over everything, while the opposite shore appeared black; but gradually the sky changed colour, as at the end of their journey, when, at the worst time possible, the *khamsin* came, hurling sand into the atmosphere. It circled far above, first in yellow-brown streaks—a bone dry, evil, crystal-sharp wind that did not, thank God, accost them out in the open; they were in safety, and could watch how it came down and swept grains of sand against the windows of the Cataract Hotel. The grains were deposited on the windowsills as piles and in the garden as little dunes, and the four of them stood at the window, looking into that insane sky which sprinkled many yellow grains—that gradually whirled Blumenberg into sleep. They covered Egypt, they covered Altenberge, they covered him, leaving nothing visible but the head of the sphinx with the broken-off nose; but as the sphinx began to speak in its hollow, almost three-thousand-year-old voice, he was already halfway to sleep and was considering the Pythagoreans, who had resisted an orientally influenced disappearance of the rational pitch system, assigning no meaning to the *hyle*, the raw sound material located between the notes determined by integral proportions of string lengths, whereas modernity was concerned precisely with exploring and listening into the intermediate realm of sounds not definable by numbers. When the commanding words of the sphinx mingled with the hyle, however, he had already fallen asleep, and remembered nothing the following day.

A Questionable Angelic Message

Emergency stop. A great shambles—a miracle that several vehicles did not all crash into one another. The police and an ambulance quickly appeared on the scene. The bloody leftovers of clothes, flesh and crushed bones scraped off the asphalt by the paramedics could no longer be recognized as a person. The truck belonging to the Zapf company had run over the body with several wheels and dragged parts of it along before stopping behind the bridge. The family, if there was one, could not be subjected to the sight of these remains. Nonetheless, the probable identity of this person could be ascertained.

The police found a white handbag in the basket of the bicycle left on the bridge, zipped up, containing one hundred and six marks and forty pfennigs, a lipstick, bits and pieces, a tampon, no key, but an ID card with the number 255431800, valid until 18 March 1984, bearing the name Elisabeth Kurz, residing at Am Schafberg, Heilbronn, 7100.

The driver and front-seat passenger of the truck were sitting in the VW police van with an officer and her colleague opposite them. They were all wet; there was a damp, clammy atmosphere in the car. The rain was still drumming on the roof.

'White like an angel,' the driver mumbled to himself. He was sweating heavily with his hands folded; they parted and he wiped his forehead, then folded them again. He was incapable of making any coherent statement. A wiry fellow with a ponytail, not one to be shaken easily. Now his right leg was trembling. Without warning, from above, not just lying on the road. 'From above,' he kept saying, rocking his head, glistening with sweat, back and forth. 'Something white.'

His eyes darted from the one officer to the other. 'On the bonnet, the bonnet first?' he asked them cluelessly.

'No—right in front of the wheels, not on the bonnet. Otherwise she'd have been sent flying.' His colleague, Harry, woollen cap pulled far down over his forehead, with blonde curls spilling out underneath it, sat there fairly quietly and stared at the table. He was grinding his teeth and making an effort not to say anything that could be taken the wrong way.

'Then down below on the right, the bang, banggg, slammed down the brakes, banggg, banggg, banggg—'

'Stepped on them full power, I can testify to that—'

He demanded that they tell him what he should have done. 'It came from above, no one expects that.'

'Ain't no one who one expects that.'

'You don't believe me?' the driver cried in despair.

Yes, they did believe him, there was nothing to suggest he was lying; but he could not believe that they believed every word, it was all so unlikely. 'From above!'

'Then a racket in the back, kind of banging. The load slipping, that's how bloody hard my colleague hit the brakes. Didn't swerve a millimetre. Couldn't have dodged anyway, he was totally in the other lane. Kept it straight as an arrow. We should check up on the load.'

The policewoman paused. The ballpoint pen she had used to record the questioning had given up the ghost. Harry reached into his breast pocket and passed her a different one, yellow with a light blue Zapf logo printed on it. It didn't write either at first, had to be breathed on, which Harry did expertly while taking another bit of paper out of his pocket and scribbling on it to try it out.

No, they were neither drunk nor overtired; their shift had only just started. And the driver didn't have a single entry in the register of traffic offenders, he had never even been in an accident. They had taken over the truck in Lüdenscheid, already loaded with furniture and boxes of books belonging to a teacher couple, their name was Blessing, B-L-E-S-S-I-N-G, that was easy to check. The couple had retired and moved to the Dollart, and now they wanted to stop off in Münster and pack some more things.

'You can't carry on driving in this state, you'd better take a break,' said the policeman. 'We'll see to it that the truck gets taken off the road and you spend the night in Münster.'

'I can take over. I'm totally calm. Nothing shaking.' Harry could no longer suppress his anger. 'We've already been stuck here for two goddamned-bloody-hours. Why do these arseholes have to kill themselves and ruin somebody else's day!' The policeman eyed him and he backpedalled: 'Didn't mean it like that.'

'Who was it anyway?' the driver asked, but the police officers couldn't give him that information as the identification was not yet complete. 'A young woman,' that was all they could say.

When Biggi returned to the apartment in the evening, she found the door half-open. No one there. No trace of the tomcat either. Her first thought was a burglary but everything was in order inside. Then she feared something terrible had happened, which was confirmed when the police called her one hour later. The tom would never appear again.

Gerhard had spent the afternoon wandering around aimlessly, finally deciding on a trip to the zoo. At the all-weather zoo, the animals dozed the time away; even the big cats seemed to be asleep in the sun, with nothing to hunt and tear apart. A tiger raised its head and yawned. The buffalo did not move, and hardly even shifted their lower jaws to chew; flamingos stood decoratively in the meadow, as fluffy as the mohair pullovers that Elke Sommer always wore in the talk shows. Only the hyper-nervous wolves ran up and down and made a bit of noise by throwing back their heads and howling, while in the opposite enclosure, a young elephant delighted children by sticking its trunk out over the barrier, searching and probing. Some words of Blumenberg's came into Gerhard's mind about the elephant that could not afford any dreams because its mass and herbivorous nature condemned it to spend all day feeding itself. Now he was already developing the same tic as Isa! Blumenbergiads at every turn. No wonder—the lecture had been captivating, spending ten minutes or more on a possible trunk culture among elephants. Spontaneous applause, hearty laughter. The professor was obviously an elephant-admirer; he seemed to feel great affection for the 'obstructed cultural companion of man', just like the children trying to reach the trunk with their little arms. It was a deep-seated sympathy for elephants probably shared by the vast majority of people in the world.

A marabou captured his attention. A bog-ugly animal, large, with a beak of rust-coloured prehistoric rock that it pressed down against its chest, its head pulled in, a bare, dirty pink neck, ghastly throat pouch and unappetising little hairs on its head—but very, very dignified as a whole. Truly a secretary from old times, versed in the arts of calligraphy, restraint and intrigue, with the stink of sweat and perfume from countless centuries beneath its dickey. Gerhard would have loved to hear what sounds the marabou made; he attempted to elicit a response from it with animal noises and a rather silly twittering, but to no avail. The marabou remained mute—and worse still, it turned away, offended, and strutted off.

There were too many mothers with children around for his taste. He was about to go, but then the sudden rain forced him to seek shelter by the crocodiles. They were lying about motionless, their eyes and nostrils barely above water.

When he arrived at the Mauritztor he found Richard already waiting for him, almost an hour early. He made a point of standing up and greeted him with a hand on his shoulder. Strange; Richard was normally far too surly for such a gesture, and never made an effort with greetings.

The Mauritztor was packed. The place was rarely frequented by students; it was too expensive. They were sitting at the cat table. Diagonally opposite, on the window side, Dietmar Schönherr and Vivi Bach were sitting in the middle of a larger round. Gerhard had both of them in direct view; he liked Dietmar Schönherr. His mother had been in love with him. As a child he had seen him on TV, in a production of *The Good Person of Szechwan*. But as what? As one of the three gods? As Shen Te or Shui Ta? The film had preoccupied him for months—how was it possible to remain good in a bad world, that whole Marxist stuff, watched over by gods. He could not help looking whenever gods appeared. Dietmar Schönherr had made a profound impression on him. He had toddled into the living room in his pyjamas. His mother was sitting on the sofa in her silk dress in honour of Dietmar Schönherr, a bottle of advocaat on the little table next to her. She did not shoo him away, but rested his head on a pillow, wrapped him in a blanket and took his feet on her lap, and they watched Dietmar Schönherr together.

'Have you heard?'

Gerhard hadn't heard anything.

Richard beckoned the waitress over and ordered him a beer. That was very bizarre too, but Gerhard refrained from asking any questions.

Richard already began telling him before the beer came. He knew most of the details—where, how and when. The news had spread quickly through Rena.

The water-seller. There was a water-seller in the play. But what was he doing there?

Richard nervously twirled a beer mat between his fingers. Gerhard kept as still as the crocodile under the surface of the swamp. His cheeks did not twitch, and his heart did not leap like a horse. When Richard paused, all he said was: 'Peace at last.'

He said no more, and carefully slurped the head off his beer.

Richard was surprised. He had never been able to stand Isa. The woman was a curse—spoilt, highfalutin, crazy, a miserable bitch. He knew how attached Gerhard was to her, how he made an ass of himself to stay near her, good-natured fool that he was. Richard had always mouthed off about Isa to pry his friend away from her, but his efforts had been in vain and he ultimately gave up. His problems with women were of an entirely different nature: the women were all after him, including some infinitely more attractive specimens than Isa, but he found it hard to make up his mind.

Wang, was the water-seller's name Wang? Over there, Schönherr raised his glass and sent a greeting into the round. Vivi Bach leaned her completely blonde head on his shoulder. Yes indeed, Wang. And Schönherr had probably played a god; darting about one of those nimble little Chinese figures would not have suited him.

Richard kept looking into his friend's eyes to see how he was taking it. It was typical of Isa that she had killed herself in such an over-the-top way. Maybe. Or maybe not. It did surprise him she had let herself be flattened. Richard felt no sympathy; what surprised him most was that Gerhard evidently didn't either, or at least there was no visible sign of it.

Richard thought it better not to mention that he had once spent a night with Isa. A tiring one. When he had started his famous boasting speech, a grumbling verbiage of seduction in the vein of Dylan, with well-calculated pauses that he always used when picking up women, she had interrupted him. Bang, cut. No more about how he got hold of Malcom Lowry's Under the Volcano at fourteen, changing the life of the Paderborn postman's son. Pfff. His flickering alcoholic existence was snuffed out and died silently inside him. Instead of listening to him and admiring his debauchedness, she kept pestering him with her Blumenberg rubbish and topped it all with more rubbish —Lacan! She wanted to go to Lacan in Paris—and no one else—for analysis. Lacan was the only one who could understand her form of madness and liberate her from Blumenberg. She had already talked her father into getting her a flat in Paris. Richard agreed sardonically: there was certainly no one in Münster who could compete with her *objet petit a*. That was year ago. Lacan died shortly afterwards.

Gerhard did not seem determined to learn all the gory details of the business. In fact, he even laughed when Richard mentioned the Zapf company. The Zapfists were brave fellows, popular with students all over the country, and now the devil had decided that dear Isa, the button girl from Heilbronn, would be dispatched by them.

The evening became a long one. Richard drank a lot, vodka and beer; he had long grown accustomed to hitting the home stretch with alcohol at night. Gerhard was not much of a drinker, but this time he was having quite a lot by his standards. The high point of the evening came when Hansi Bitzer, the poem monster, entered the joint. Richard couldn't stand him, and entrenched himself grumpily behind his beer. Hansi made for their table and planted himself in front of Gerhard; Richard could have throttled him. 'In the Air Tonight' by Phil Collins was coming out of the speakers, which did not stop Hansi from getting out his stupid mag, one of those wank mags wrapped in transparent plastic; he took it out of his accordion portfolio and started singing in a croaking, rattling voice, right into the ethereal bustle of Collins and the general chattering racket, and directly into Gerhard's ears:

Now then! So I'm rid of you,
You cheeky, licentious wench!
A curse on your sinful womb,
A curse on your venal, lustful body,
A curse on your whorish breasts
Devoid of discipline or truth,
Heavy with shame and lies,
A dirty pillow for all loathsome desires . . .

Jesus bloody Christ! It went on and on, endlessly, endlessly. A punitive sermon? Directed at poor Gerhard to console him for his loss with anger and contempt? Gerhard listened attentively, at any rate, and not a muscle in his face gave away what he was thinking. Once Hansi had finished, he reached somewhat ceremoniously for his wallet, pulled out a smooth tenner, folded it twice and laid it in Hansi's tin. Hansi left it at a small bow, turned around and left without wasting a single glance on Dietmar Schönherr.

'Who does he think he is?'

Richard saw it as his duty to protect his friend after the fact, but he didn't know his Gerhard, his dear, good old Gerhard, as well as he thought:

'If you cut your throat, And jump into the Spree, You'll never find a grave, For the chaff rises to the top' Gerhard quoted, gurgling cheerfully, 'Now that's class, that's the really, really big, oversized weight class, the poetic heavyweight class'—he started giggling, swallowing some beer by accident—'None of our feckless, well-behaved poet-posers would dare write like that any more. Rühmkorf, for example? Huh? Gernhardt?!'

Richard had to smile, but remained concerned and decided to keep an eye on his friend that night. His actual reason for wanting to meet up was not mentioned; Richard wanted to skip two semesters and go on a big trip to South America.

Heilbronn

Her parents heard the news from a Heilbronn policeman who appeared at their door that same evening. They couldn't believe it. They demanded evidence and phoned their daughter's flat in desperation, but could only reach a sobbing Biggi; they froze.

For a long time, they were unable to shake off their torpor. Cold on the outside. Hot on the inside. Thoughts racing through their minds. And their little sweetie-pie kept appearing in them, their darling. They had reckoned with all sorts of bad things, but not that. How? Their little girl, whom they had given everything that parents could ever give a child, had done something like that? Had she done it to destroy her parents? But what guilt had they incurred to be repaid with such horror? Had Elisabeth been under the influence of drugs? That was not the child they knew. Perhaps they had been too soft on the child, they had been stricter with the two boys; but that was no reason to kill oneself, let alone in such a frightful way that they refused to think of it—their youngest of all people, such a cheerful, clever, wild child who found everything easy, kindergarten, school, even dancing lessons, and God knows that was a drag for young people, and university even more. Their darling had even looked sweet in puberty, not covered in spots like the other two. And she could do whatever she wanted, they had never interfered by telling her what subject to study. Philosophy, that sounded interesting, even if they did not quite know what a course like that was good for; but if Elisabeth wanted that, then certainly she should have what she desired. Where on earth did it come from? Their marriage was not a bad one, they had never burdened the children with their own problems. Did it come from Uncle Willi? But Willi had been in the war and hadn't come to terms with life afterwards; it was a result of war. So where, where did it come from?

The funeral took place ten days later at the main cemetery in Heilbronn. The Protestant vicar did his job well, though there was no way to make things better. One could hear the helplessness in his voice. Elisabeth had been in his confirmation class, and he remembered the girl very well: she was clever, unpredictable and lively, and rather serious for such a young thing. Could ask difficult questions aimed right at the heart of the thorny mass of theological logic. The vicar had no choice but to portray her death as an unsolved riddle, refraining from overly unctuous emphasis on his verses of compassion. Scarcely possible to take any of the burden off her parents' shoulders. They sat in the front row, stiff as two candles, one long and one short.

Gerhard had joined the funeral procession at the back. The brown coffin, held slightly crookedly by the black-uniformed bearers, the wreaths dragged along—for him, the things he saw had no connection to Isa. How little whatever was lying in there resembled Isa. She had definitely not slipped into a friend-peopled sleep. She had made short work: a doll, broken. Twice and thrice over.

It was not as if the love of his life had departed and he now had to waste away with grief. From one moment to the next, Isa had become alien to him, disturbingly alien. He had been fooled by a cruel ghost dressed up as a young girl. He felt a terrible thirst. He was seized by a cough that made his eyes water. Wrinkled monkey-face, wiped dry by his jacket sleeve; his smooth cheeks and smooth forehead, furrowed. Isa, or whatever was left of her, watched him. Isa's seawater eyes looked with sympathy at the little monkey. A grim rapture came over him. He ran his hand over a box tree and pinched off a leaf. Busy sparrows underneath, peck, peck, peck. Two fat ones with baby fluff on their chests. Little souls that die faster than they hatch. He thought of Isa's chubby hands—always ready to withdraw. No, it was her, the love of his life, Springsteen's 'Suicide Machine'. She gripped his very being. Willing flutter of kisses in his head, a craving without rhyme or reason. He wished he were back in that accursed iron bed. But perhaps it was better for such a domineering love to be driven out of one's being. One should love in a good, conscientious and reasonable way and seek a modest peace, a modest happiness. He would not stew in his pain forever. He was alive, and the dead lay mute in their graves or stood in the passage to nowhere.

The procession came to a halt under three tall pines. Several wheelbarrows stood by the side path. A pair of satyrines disappeared in their shadow. A little side note: his outfit was ridiculously serious. His shoes squeezed his feet.

The next day her parents received guests in their home. For God's sake, they asked, why had Isa never introduced them to this sweet, decent person whom they took into their hearts immediately, in so far as they were still able? They would have done anything to make Gerhard feel at ease there, and would—discreetly, of course, one mustn't interfere too much—have made it clear to Elisabeth that he was the right one for her. Gerhard would make something of himself, old Kurz saw at once, and money was not an issue anyway; they had enough money themselves.

When Gerhard entered the spacious house, where the parents were standing around like lonely, timid birds, barely able to offer him a place on the sofa with a firm voice—how hard her mother's hand trembled as she held it out to pour him a cup of tea and push a little flower-adorned plate of shortbread towards him—he understood Isa even less.

She was as small as an elf, very delicate. Compost-coloured little shoes, size 34.

'Sugar?'

'No thank you, no sugar.'

He had expected cold, haughty, ostentatious people, but they were different. They were not the sort of parents who put their children through hell, they were understanding people who had been deprived of everything they believed in. Their faces were the colour of pickled artichokes. They made an effort to seem level-headed and looked at him with shy expectation, her father with Isa's seawater eyes and her mother as if in a trance. Did they think he would come there as their daughter's avenger and give them a stern lecture? He didn't know what he was doing there himself, and felt like an intruder.

It was difficult to sit properly on the giant sofa; he bent his finger and dug around for a cigarette in the empty packet that he had drawn from his trouser pocket, fluff and all, until old Kurz saved him by offering a Roth-Händle and snapping open his lighter. The ashtray had a button on top; when it was pushed, the lid moved and one dropped the ash into its dark belly.

A likeable old codger. He constantly walked back and forth, stroked the armrests of the armchairs and gave a touchingly ceremonious speech about his little girl. The Messiah could not have been wiser than the child, nor the Queen of Sheba more delightful. Suddenly his face took on a pinched expression, and he had to turn away to weep silently to himself. He blew his nose and his pain into a chequered handkerchief.

Her armchair stood far away from the coffee table. She pulled herself up a little. In a soft, stretched voice like a damp cloth: 'Please help us. What was the matter with our Elisabeth?'

Gerhard searched for the right way to begin. 'She was strange, sometimes even more than strange. Exultant, yes, then strangely quiet. Everything in rapid succession. But she didn't have anything to do with drugs or alcohol. Nothing worth mentioning, at least. Blumenberg—'

'What about Blumenberg?' she interrupted. 'It seems she was completely bewitched by him. Please tell us, what exactly was going on there? What her friends told us sounded worrying.'

'No, the professor certainly never touched her, absolutely not, you can be sure of that; Isa never even spoke to him. No one believed in a genuine affair. Blumenberg probably didn't even know that she was studying with him; she never went to see him.'

'And there's nothing you haven't told us?' her father asked with unexpected severity. 'You're not trying to cover for the professor, are you?' With the best will in the world, he could not imagine his Elisabeth being in love with a man who hadn't even noticed her. Out of the question. His sweetie-pie turned everyone's heads, not the other way around.

'And what else? There must have been something.' Everything was in a muddle inside Isa's mother, but a slow and laborious one. That was probably the medication.

He felt like a bad psychologist, and failed miserably. Waffled about instability, mood swings, demonstrative absence, how often she was somewhere else, far, far away. Hard to say what was really going on inside her. But there were no dramatic events as far as he knew.

A wide room with a low ceiling. In front of the windows, an interminably long console stretching from one wall to the other; on it stood a stately brass clock whose glass casing had a glass pendulum swinging inside it, as well as two Chinese vases shielded by cream-coloured lampshades. Carpets everywhere. A beige four-seater couch, on which he was sitting alone, and three beige armchairs. A wooden propeller from an old aeroplane hanging from the rear wall. Along the wall, a bookshelf with art books, vases, odds and ends, a miniature of Michelangelo's *David*, some non-fiction books and a few novels—Grass and Walser, he had seen in passing, *Gone with the Wind*, *To Kill a Mockingbird*. Tasteful, yes. Ostentatious, definitely not.

Silence spread, penetrated by the striking of the pendulum clock on the console—three times, four times, five times. It sounded loud when Gerhard let the ashtray snap shut.

'Please tell us more, please don't stop.' It sounded like pleading. The mother wanted to escape the silence, or perhaps she just wanted to be comforted by another voice; he was unsure if she was even listening to him. Her light brown, silky eyes, glazed over with too much or too little emotion, kept drifting off into space.

He felt burnt-up, as if someone had pointed a flamethrower at his skull. Now he was sitting there with a pile of ash in his brain. He needed feelings to think properly, feelings to say something precise. All he could think of was the time Isa screamed 'Go fuck yourself!' at him. At a crazed volume. Images of mashed bones and blood-stained shreds of a white dress wandered about before his inner eye. A meteor crashed through the ceiling and landed smoking on the carpet. He could not possibly offer that to Isa's parents. What he told them about her life in the shared flat sounded lifeless, as if cardboard people had lived there: with cardboard furniture in a cardboard flat with a cardboard tomcat, and while he strung together one cardboard thought after another, it turned six o'clock and it was time to go.

The Lion III

Blumenberg learnt of what had happened from the news-paper two days later, but remained ignorant of his own part in the drama. There was talk of the case among his colleagues at the university, certainly, but because he had never had any direct contact with his student and not even known her name, he did not connect the tragedy to the young woman who had always sat upright in the front row, a rather slight figure; nor did he ask himself why she had suddenly disappeared and never returned.

He spent the night and another night reading, com-piling index cards and dictating. Things around him had quietened down again. He had returned to his usual amount of work, even an excess of work. The lion had meanwhile become indispensable. Conversely, it also seemed to have grown used to him. It slept calmly on the rug like an old house dog, only rarely lifting its head to assess the situation. And it had not grown emaciated, not turned to skin and bone. Old, to be sure, but otherwise unchanged.

The moon was full. Its light, borrowed from the sun, delicately glazed the bushes and trees. When Blumenberg looked out of the window, his will—just as Schopenhauer formulated—began to disappear from consciousness, replaced by a calm in his heart that was difficult to achieve in other ways. The mild moonlight was beautiful because humans have nothing to do with the moon. If one credited it with being the worldly eye of a god, then this eye gazed down at the earth leniently and indifferently.

When he saw the moon, he automatically thought of the famous lines by Matthias Claudius, and hummed them inwardly along with the words that entered his head of their own accord. He particularly loved these:

The forest stands black and silent
And the white mist rises
Wondrously from the meadows.

The moon and the black, silent forest were drawn into the human lifeworld, where, through the power of metaphors, they could take root with great intensity and dwell meaningfully inside, whether a person had ever wandered about in the black woods or not. The second stanza of Claudius' song was perfectly suited to him, it was his very own stanza, encompassing his life in the enclosure of his study, even if the sleeping away it invoked usually remained unattainable:

How still is the world tonight
And in the shell of twilight
So intimate and fair.

As a silent room
In which the misery of day
Can be forgotten and slept away.

And yet. And yet. As soon as he turned away from the window, Blumenberg had to admit that he had a stronger influence than the moon in his study, a tremendous one even, that pulled him out of a world in which the facts of experience applied, pervaded and seized by logical thought. Remoulding matter into the pure phenomenon, removing all substances that normally belonged to it— was that possible? Could such a thing even exist? Sometimes he was overcome with distrust and felt that all the words he spoke into the patiently winding dictaphone tapes night after night were dead words, dead, dead, dead, because they did not apply to the creature on the carpet.

He loved his lion. Much the same as a child loves its dog. He recalled the magical photo of Glenn Gould, a handsome youth sitting at the grand piano with his black-and-white spotted dog, an equally handsome dog, looking intently at the opened sheet music with its paws resting on the keys alongside the pianist's fingers. It seemed as if the two of them were playing together—as if Glenn Gould could, in fact, only achieve what he did thanks to the dog's collaboration.

His lion was less good-natured and of a less burlesque disposition, but a mighty protector. A dream birth of such absolute presence that he could have leaned against its side and drifted off into an everlasting sleep.

But no. Not a dream. The lion was ultimately such a free and absolute creature that no one could challenge its right to be what it expressed itself as being. Its satisfaction at being emanated from its by now slightly flimsy lion costume in self-luminous projection; it was pointless to assail this thing that showed itself on the rug with ever new doubts. With this fabulously lion-like chimera, which could perhaps only be distinguished from a genuine lion by touching it with one's own hands, the great orchestrator and knot-tangler—if HE indeed existed, eternal and unseen, but working in secret—had tied an especially magnificent knot. The key was to delight in it: plunge in and enjoy the flow of power rising at your feet and enveloping you.

Blumenberg had still not attempted the hand test. Even without it there were still slim, fragile points of contact between him and the lion. It did not cost him any great effort to imagine feeling the lion's fur against his cheek, feeling the lion's paw against his shoulder. When he felt such contact he was released from the necessity of radical self-disposal. There was something profoundly calmative about the softening of physical reality in conjunction with a being that blossomed unwaveringly into the phenomenal. Not that he could no longer be held responsible for anything; but the things that had been placed on his shoulders now felt light, as fluffy as the chest fur of a young sparrow.

Although, sometimes when he was deep in thought and looked up from the table, he got almost as much of a shock as he had the first time. Then the immensity of the lion returned with full force. A lion! A miracle! A lion! His heart soon calmed down but his thoughts began to spin, and a feeling that fluctuated between fear and delight made him look upwards with furrowed brow, though he saw only the ceiling there and no heavenly vista. Perhaps everything he wrote and thought was surveyed, commented on and controlled from above? Perhaps he, the night watchman, was watched over by another night, gifted with a penetrating intelligence, that had sent him the lion for encouragement, or perhaps to make him finally write more clearly, uncompromisingly and resolutely, to make him take risks and commit his utmost to paper?

In such moments he saw himself cracking a whip, driving along a gaggle of theologians. He grew lion's teeth. The sacrifice of Isaac! Harrrrrr! God had not released the sacrifice from his binds to warn men and make them abandon such sacrifices—no, the ram was not made to stand in for purposes of civilizing humans; rather, HE disdained the sacrifice of Isaac because it was *too meagre*. Isaac, the little creature, the insignificant son, much too insignificant for a sacrifice to God. HE had waited for the greater sacrifice, had craved it, HE had planned the sacrifice of his own son! But why? To augment the emotional uniformity of the divine, which had so far contained at most anger and zeal, with pain, to experience suffering himself and feel something like a father's pain? He thought of the alabaster trinity by Hans

Multscher with the face of God the Father dismayed, dismayed by what had come to pass.

Or: when the call for Barabbas sounded in the passion, what the people said in Aramaic was in fact *Bar-Abbas*, 'son of the father', which meant that the Jews were demanding back Jesus, their king, from the hands of Pilate and had remained loyal—as opposed to the catastrophic interpretation that took it as the call to release a criminal.

When such thoughts came over him, he felt the blood flowing freshly through his veins; everything inside him tingled and circulated for all it was worth. At those times he could barely stay in his chair, and had to pace about in his room or stand at his high desk for a while and perform squats, albeit at an appropriate distance from the lion, which rather limited his leeway for movement. The lion, which at least raised its head during such manoeuvres and gazed at him—slightly worriedly, it seemed to him, or perhaps ironically?—with bemused lion's eyes. Once or twice he had even wished he had claws and paws instead of hands and fingernails along with a muscle-swollen, fur-covered body to have a royal romp with the lion. How divine to roar with a lion and playfully sink his teeth into its flank; his hands were actually twitching in an effort to stimulate the growth of claws. And he was slightly furry himself; when he looked at his delicate hands, then at the hairs spilling out from under his pushed-back knitted cuffs, he felt a proximity to lions.

He had once stood in front of a cage and watched a lion and lioness mating. At close range. An incredible spectacle, an assault on the ears. The roaring reverberated so loudly off the tiled walls that he had to shield his ears with his hands. The lion was young, in its prime, a magnificent animal that roared from its innermost core. The shiny fur, the play of muscles—enchanting. And terrifying at the same time. Paw strokes, bites to the nape. The lioness was pushed down with power. It was violent, obscene, far exceeding all human drives. Blumenberg shuddered and could not bear the sight for long. Two children stood next to him and watched the spectacle open-mouthed, standing stiff like little pillars of salt.

Once he had calmed down and was sitting in his chair again, he became cheerful and very, very peaceful. The heavenly space from which the lion had poured down, constituting itself as a deceptively authentic manifestation and dozing on the carpet with a very natural look to it, was there to bolster his, Blumenberg's, faith in the world, at least by night.

The night invited memory. With the withdrawal and muting of all urgent sounds, things that had been covered up emerged and encountered the inner sensory organs. But the lion ensured that it happened without fear. Early in the morning, when his voice no longer filled the room while in contact with the dictaphone, he often returned to the camp in Zerbst. Dances of death. Not entirely dissolved, it now approached him in a lighter floating manner. He no longer lay trembling, hungry and in a cold sweat on a bug-infested wooden plank bed. He no longer smelt the breathtaking stench. The lion protected him

from fear of death. The lion brought Heinrich Dräger to
him, the Lübeck industrialist who rescued him from the
camp and later funded his university studies. Dräger's
astute eyes rested on him. Diving lungs, high-altitude
breathing apparatuses and gas masks had been manufactured in the Dräger factories. It was difficult to breath at
that time. Whatever remained of the camp had to pass
the lion's guard; this ensured retrospection in digestible
doses. There may have been a little bird fluff hanging on
the barbed wire, but not a mangled human form. The
wire itself had turned into a hook pattern that could no
longer mutilate a body. The Todt Organisation. When the
name went through the lion, it lost its evil radiance. Runway construction for jet planes. Casting metal plates for
the Autobahn. He didn't have to fill in joints any more.
Cutting peat. He didn't have to cut peat any more. His
hands were no longer torn and bloody. What he took on
his shovel now was light. Light papers on which he
researched the pathologies of the time. First-degree
Mischling. The nasty term had become harmless. His
mother's three sisters, who were murdered in Theresien-
stadt, and also Laura, his favourite aunt, no longer pointed
their fingers at him as someone who could enjoy his life
in peace. Whatever lay in the shadows partook of the air's
enfolding breath, and those who had separated from life
fled further into the darkening air.

He had practised redemptive statements in the camp.
He once received a postcard adorned with the sleeping
lion by Christian Daniel Rauch. Not its wakeful brother.

The two monumental metal fellows came from the lion school of the Hohenzollern family; they had lain at the entrance of the hotel *Stadt Hamburg*. In the night of Palm Sunday 1942 they disappeared, and when everything was over they resurfaced in the little complex in front of the Holsten Gate. The tired lion slept, its inclined head resting on one paw: there was nothing mane-like about its mane, which resembled a wig made of tassels and corkscrews. In his childhood, one test of courage was to sneak past the hotel porter and climb onto one of the shining backs until the porter noticed and chased them away. In the camp the lion's deep sleep had preoccupied him. And a childlike idea came to him: if the lion wakes up, I am saved. The steel-biting lion would tear open its jaws and chew up his enemies.

His carpet lion was not made of black cast iron. Its mane showed no lack of manefulness. A true dialogue between him and the lion had not yet taken place, even though they were always within earshot of each other. The lion did not open its jaws and utter royal words in rough-voiced, perfect German. It did, however, yawn now and then. Or perhaps it only opened its mouth to air its teeth and to show that in an emergency, it was still in charge of the situation and could tear the uncontrollably real into the room with a swipe of its paw.

He had made an effort not to burden anyone with the fear he had once felt, and which later returned on some nights. 'Do not play with another person's depths'—he had intuitively attempted to follow this Wittgenstein's command, even if he did not always succeed. One had to protect the other from one's own fear, and also avoid wilfully eliciting the other's fear. Declaring one's own fear would only put the other person in an awkward position. The lion was an other that could bear a greater burden. If he was now overcome by fear, he passed it on without reservations to the lion, which understood and simultaneously defused it.

Blumenberg conversed with it through inner speech and listening; this was no less intense than an exchange between them that could be taped would have been. The lion heard everything, assessed everything and paid attention to Blumenberg's dictations, with majestic ears that could even hear thoughts discarded in an embryonic state and eyes that did not miss the slightest movement, to ensure that the philosopher remained on course in the aerial manoeuvres of his intellect.

The lion did not function as Wittgenstein had believed. 'If a lion could speak, we could not understand it,' he had claimed. Blumenberg certainly understood it. The lion acted as a confidence generator that lightly smoothed down the hairs of protest that kept standing up in Blumenberg's thought. Whenever Blumenberg was about to set off a false alarm, he saw the lion give a twitch that interrupted and terminated the still semi-articulated thought. If he was at risk of resting for too long on empty phrases, if his words became inflated with useless flourishes and ornaments, the lion immediately communicated its disapproval and the air went out of the intellectual balloon. Blumenberg then cleared his throat apologetically and said nothing. For a second, his brain sank into a glimmering blackness before resurfacing with radiant clarity, ready for a new statement—one about theology, for example. He dictated with incisive relish, 'a swaggering before the hidden majesty, an objection to the self-withdrawal of the divinity'. As he did so he was seized by the urge to laugh, for he suddenly saw himself with the lion, parading up and down in a zigzag before the hidden majesty.

The lion exerted a further influence on him: when he had thought of his academic colleagues in the past, there had sometimes been petty stirrings of envy. Envy towards his colleague Habermas in particular, who was extremely influential and had bred an impressive battalion of pupils. Habermas—one heard the name all over the country. To be sure, he had always found his niggling envy ignoble and useless, resulting from an idiotic devaluation of himself that he should long since have overcome; he had not managed to shake it off, however, especially because his colleague had the same publisher and his books had a far greater turnover than his own. Since being graced the lion's company, he was free of such petty jealousies. Habermas could do whatever he wanted; it no longer mattered to him—in fact, he even acknowledged Habermas' efforts with cheerful frivolity whenever he encountered them in the newspaper. He had also developed an aversion to his colleague Taubes, whom he had initially regarded highly and who had given him impulses for his own work on various occasions. The man could hear the grass growing on people's desks. But his swindling talent, his penchant for intrigue and attacks, his critical posturing and the muddled circumstances into which he manoeuvred had gradually soured Blumenberg's relationship with him. His replies to Taubes' last few letters had been frosty. Filtered through the lion, his colleague's badness was no longer a source of vexation but the morose windmill battle of a haunted, disturbed soul incapable of standing by what he said, and was more worthy of pity than damnation. Nonetheless, even with the lion, he could not convince himself to revive their contact.

The lion had alleviated a further vexation: whereas typographical errors that he found in his writings had formerly sent him into a rage—on one occasion, he had opened a freshly printed book and immediately caught sight of 'bock', 'bock' instead of 'book', just imagine, and that devilry had ruined his entire Christmas—they still annoyed him, but only for a short time; in fact, he secretly developed a feeling for the amusing hidden meanings in such errors, though he gave no inkling to others, to those responsible, so as to avoid tempting them to make even more mistakes. He liked to refer to himself as a 'lucky opener', meaning someone who could open a book to the part most essential for him the first time he touched it. In the case of 'bock', he had been more of an unlucky opener.

No more absurd commotions, no more games of confusion. The lion helped establish clarity and trust, in the small personal things as well as the larger ones. As if

Augustine's doctrine of illuminations, the divine revelation of the ground of being, had entered his room soft-footedly to take root there. Something of the world's favour granted to him as a child had returned to him as an adult with a brilliant mind, nurtured by and trained in modern scepticism. He could now effortlessly be a Ptolemaian and a Copernican at once; he wandered about between the two ways of interpreting the world like a visitor marvelling at two splendidly furnished halls, one with a closed roof and the other with a hole in it.

In secret, an inexhaustible assurance flowed from the lion that the net of names cast over heaven and earth by humans to calm themselves would remain tear-resistant even when physicists, astronomers, biologists and philological dissectors busily scratched and cut away at every name and every metaphor conjured up by it with fine scissors and scrapers. This did not mean that the truth was a static given. It had to change, but more in the form of gradual metamorphoses, without a rigid disintegration of older ascriptions and thought models that were sent to kingdom come.

Although everything was now arranged to his satisfaction, he sometimes caught himself in a reverie about presenting his lion to a gathering of zoologists in a giant auditorium. Like an animal tamer, albeit without a whip, he entered with the lion creeping along behind him. He bent down and whispered his orders into its ear, commanded it to sit on its hind legs or lie down, to roll on its back and show its belly. The experts were baffled, very baffled indeed when, after he had urged them to perform the hand test, they carefully moved closer and—each letting the other go first—reached straight through the lion, literally grasping only a handful of nothing.

Hansi

A lecture had been cancelled because the professor was ill. Some took it as a sign that this illness was connected to the death of his student. For as long as they could remember, the professor had never cancelled a lecture. The students waited to see if he would make any mention of the incident in the coming weeks, if only in some distant allusion.

In tense anticipation, Hansi sat in his seat with his notebook open and his Montblanc pen laid across it, a solitary between three vacant seats that were avoided as if one would catch a rash by sitting there. Although the lecture theatre filled up and some were already squatting on the floor, no one sat down next to Hansi. It was very rare for him to have a neighbour, and when he did it was always one of the elderly people from the city, who didn't know him.

This time Gerhard sat down next to him, which gave Hansi a tiny start; his left cheek began to twitch.

'Who wrote "Pontus Euxinus"?' Gerhard asked.

Hansi moved slightly away from him, but answered in a clear voice: 'An unknown student who died in the detention room.' Then he picked up his leather portfolio off the floor, rummaged about inside it and took out the sheet with the poem on it. He placed it in front of Gerhard.

Gerhard skimmed over the page. It was neatly typed, presumably on Hansi's typewriter, in slightly curved, somewhat girlish lettering.

'And how did you find it?'

Richard sat down on Gerhard's left without greeting Hansi. Hansi ignored it and kept his head straight, observing Gerhard only from the corner of his eye and beginning an extended monologue about his poetic research: he had discovered temperaments that insisted on the special privilege of concealment, whether out of indifference or resignation, and he saw it as his duty to preserve and protect their carefully created incognito, only giving the poetry itself freedom and helping it to have an effect. It was all the more remarkable when the poems that had once been cast onto paper in hasty scribblings, without any claim to eternity, had miraculously been preserved and now found in him, Hansi, someone who could make their voices heard again and thus fulfil their true destiny.

Gerhard had difficulty concentrating on Hansi, as Richard kept babbling at him from the left. He was likewise a great blusterer, and was telling Gerhard about his South-American plans.

Then the side door opened; Blumenberg entered and took off his hat and coat.

Gerhard only understood Blumenberg's first few sentences. They dealt with the subjunctive as a masterful instrument for bringing different times towards thought in the irrealis in order to counteract time captivated with the help of measuring instruments, as well as that which had deposited itself in memories as expired time, and hence an apparently secure store, and converting it into other models. Blumenberg had wiped the central field of the enormous, not-quite-clean blackboard behind him, written the word 'irrealis' and drawn numerous lines extending outwards from it, making it look like a hedgehog.

Gerhard could not read the words written away from the lines to the right or those written towards them on the left, as he was short-sighted. Blumenberg's explanations also became blurred inside him, or at best surfaced in fragments, because Isa was cycling past him in her white dress again and again.

Though Blumenberg also spoke of the dead—who lie in wait for the living in the background as witnesses, witnesses to whom the living must justify themselves, which brought up the idea of immortality, as ever-new generations were causing an extension of time beyond the deaths of the recently deceased that drifted off into the eternal, and here the subjunctive brought its subtle exploratory possibilities to this constantly and infinitely extended time, especially with regard to witness—the professor's deliberations could scarcely be related to the recent fatality. Gerhard suspected that Blumenberg was unaware who the dead student was, and could not see the slightest connection to himself. Secretly he resented him. Even if Blumenberg had not played any active part in whatever he had represented in Isa's brain, it was a professor-puppet named Blumenberg that had chased her to her death, or at least hastened her decision. Time and again he heard the striking of the clock that stood on the console in the living room of Isa's parents.

Hansi too was evidently having a hard time concentrating, perhaps because of the unusual circumstance that a fellow student had occupied the seat next to him. He desperately kept his notebook shut to prevent Gerhard from gaining unauthorized insight into it. When he opened it to note something down, he used only the right page and lifted up the left so that his scribbling would remain secret. His legs kept swinging apart and together in a scissor motion until he placed a hand on his right thigh and brought the movement under control.

Richard was very relaxed in his seat; it would probably not take very long for him to fall asleep entirely. While the man on the right was sitting bolt upright like a pharaoh, the man on his left was slumping down more and more. Gerhard felt awkward trapped between two such dissimilar neighbours. Though it was Hansi who was more of a problem; he regretted sitting down next to him. Hansi exuded an incredible tension that also affected him, putting his entire right side in a state of excitement—not a productive excitement, for example, the kind that made him more attentive but rather an aggressive, paranoid discord that now began to rage inside him too.

Gerhard just barely managed to pick up one sentence —'If the dead could still smile, Stefan George would have smiled'—which Blumenberg read as showing that the subjunctive offered an extraordinarily subtle view of the soul, that it offered *noble-mindedness*; then Gerhard's attention was gone. Hansi had him in his grip. All his thoughts revolved around Hansi and attempted to fathom the phenomenon of Hansi.

Why was it so complicated to get along with Hansi? Gerhard was not the only one who found it difficult, even though he had just received an astonishing proof of trust from this strange fellow in the form of a sheet with the poem on it. Hansi was handsome, perhaps the most handsome man in Münster. Not only more handsome than all the men in *Tatort*—which wasn't saying much—but also more handsome than most Hollywood actors. He drew looks—amazed, thoughtful and agitated ones. But only for a short while. Something was amiss with Hansi; he was perched somewhere high, high above. And he had the peculiar habit, extinct among students, of always eating with a napkin tucked down his front.

Gerhard looked at Hansi's left hand and saw a ring he had never noticed before, fashioned from two slender stylized hands whose fingers were interlocked. The ring was handsome too. But Hansi's fingertips were stained brown from smoking.

Hansi was lonelier than any other student in Münster, Gerhard was sure of that. He was of tall build but not too tall, slim but not bony, and his well-groomed brown-black hair went down to his neck. He had sharply defined blue eyes, a bold yet delicate-winged nose that would have made Lavater effuse, and an immaculately formed chin that was not too soft and not too energetic. He wore dark blue jackets with a captain's flair, always in perfect condition; he probably had them tailor-made, for they fit his shoulders perfectly in exactly the way that was the norm in men's clothing for a long time. Hansi did not go along with the fashion of overhanging padded shoulders. And there was nothing about him that needed padding; Hansi was most handsome when his manly clothes sparsely covered him without any creasing or pinching. If anything he wore was fashionable it was his tight jeans, neither faded nor patched nor ripped. And dark brown leather shoes to go with them, never Clarks and never sneakers. Hansi was undoubtedly a man with a gentleman's attitude, but this attitude led nowhere.

Hansi was very clean; his hair was always freshly washed and he kept his fingernails perfectly white. He smelt good. Why did Gerhard avoid him, why did his fellow students avoid him?

No one had ever seen him in an intimate relationship, either with a man or a woman. It was generally assumed that Hansi was gay, but too shy to come out of hiding. Maybe, maybe not. There was no theory with the slightest claim to any verifiable truth.

Hansi remained an enigma to everyone. Someone suspected that his family came from Switzerland. This theory was supported by his elevated German, which had occasional Helveticisms. He lodged with a 'slumber mother wearing an anti-snoring band', Hansi had once quipped, causing a noticeable stir—until it was found out that 'slumber mother' referred to his landlady. Every night for months, Hansi's fellow students subsequently bedded him next to an anti-snoring band until the joke gradually wore off. It seemed likely that he came from a fairly affluent family, as he lived in a villa in the most expensive part of Münster. His only association with love came from the poems he either read from the page or recited from memory.

Time after time, Gerhard had opportunity to observe women trying to get close to Hansi. Some of them had set themselves the task of saving Hansi and restoring him to the human community as an immaculate beau, but even the most persistent eventually had to admit that in Hansi's case, they were barking up the wrong tree. Whoever came into contact with him did not, at any rate, elicit what could be called an emotional response. His indifference was impenetrable. Feelings expressed to him were absorbed without a trace. Isa had candidly told Gerhard how handsome she found Hansi, and that she been attracted to him and then immediately repelled again. When she encountered him for the first time at Blumenberg's lecture, she secretly eyed him and reached a very favourable judgement, but quickly became suspicious: there was something wrong with Hansi. He had a screw loose.

His tic with the poems! Hansi regularly turned up at restaurants; in the summer he contented himself with performances on the street, and in the winter he pushed his way indoors, made for two or three neighbouring tables and let rip. He fixed his ice-cold gaze on his victims, asking for permission with a token phrase and proceeding without an answer, began to deliver poems in an unpleasantly shrill tone. He knew most of them by heart, and for a few he took sheets out of plastic pockets from his portfolio, looked at the paper, then looked at his listeners, who were sitting in their chairs with defensive expressions as if nailed to them, and became a source of torment for everyone, absolutely everyone.

A few who didn't know him were surprised that the man was so handsome yet so twisted, while others who had often heard him grew downright wild. It sometimes happened that people threw slices of tomato at Hansi, or that the menu landed at his feet like a wobbly aeroplane; a furious woman even threw a peppermill at him once. Most waiters didn't dare to chase him out of their establishments. He went up to the tables with such determination that significant damage might have ensued if someone had sought to prevent it. At the end of his presentation, Hansi bowed and collected money in a dented Gitanes tin ashtray. The pickings were meagre. His fellow students were also baffled by his strange way of begging; Hansi could not possibly have needed the few pfennigs he gathered like this.

The poems he recited all dealt with love or, more precisely, the struggle of love. And they were certainly no inferior ones—Friedrich Hölderlin, Johann Wolfgang von Goethe and Clemens von Brentano all had the dubious honour of being brought to a fatal minute-long life by Hansi's hellish voice on the tiny restaurant stages of the city of Münster. Hansi omitted the names of the authors, but no one was interested in learning who had written them anyway.

Hansi evidently loved poems in which a fluttering 'I' had to encircle, enclose, hunt down or eternally abandon a great 'You'. The truly peculiar part sometimes came at the end of his performance, though by then not a single ear was willing to listen—Hansi closed with a poem full of riddles, as dark as its author, who had disappeared into darkness:

> And a stone for me and a stone for you
> at the dark Pontus Euxinus,
> and here and there a stork's leg
> and seventeen pennies less.
> Of the sabre cut no more than an eighth
> of drunken janissaries,
> in the red evening sky the trail of birds
> from nine-and-ninety years.
>
> The whale and the nightingale
> with forty rubber balls,
> and a ball for me and a ball for you
> in the battle of the Dardanelles.
> The rose with the slave's thorn,

the sparrow hawk sings vigils,
and here and there on the Golden Horn
the Islam of Sicily.

And all the circles black and red,
the radish flowers in Spain,
and bread for me and bread for you
and the chestnuts for Lotte.
Welcome, bitter sunshine
in the steam of the foggy seas,
and here and there a stork's leg
and honour to God alone.

Gerhard was maybe the only person who could listen to
Hansi without a vehement expression of displeasure. The
voice repelled him as much the others, but he found it a
curious endeavour to wander from each table to the next
as a living bard, and so he patiently observed Hansi to
study the phenomenon. A young man with respect for
poems! That was highly unusual, and even bordered on
the improbable. Gerhard had identified the authors of the
poems immediately, except for the last one, whose tone
was foreign to his ears and aroused his curiosity.

Although almost an hour had passed and Richard had
indeed fallen asleep, Hansi was still sitting in the same
tense, defensive posture, and stayed exactly the same
when Gerhard slid the Euxinus poem back to him. Hansi's
arm twitched as if he had been given an electric shock.
Then he packed the paper away without comment.

Gerhard tried to imagine what Hansi's face would look like in a few years: completely frozen, with thinning, but equally long hair and hard furrows around his mouth. Maybe he would have developed some quirks; his cheek twitch, for example, would have got completely out of control. And perhaps, despite all the cleanliness Hansi displayed now, he would even be missing a few teeth. He then thought of the achievements of the subjunctive lauded by the professor a while ago, but the lecture had long since moved on to other subjects.

The Lion IV

He was not satisfied with the lecture. He found it somewhat disjointed; he had not been able to display his narrative talent as brilliantly as usual. The lion had remained
absent, and that had made him uneasy and deprived him
of one or two good ideas. Upon returning to his study he
found the lion there as usual, thank God. This time he
had not managed to find a good way of ending before dis-
missing his listeners. Perhaps his failure was also due to
the fact that he had suffered a bout of flu and been forced
to spend two days in bed. Illnesses, he hated illnesses.
They were not for him. They were for people who liked
to crawl away into their beds and whimper to themselves.

His mood suffered; he still felt a slight lack of energy.
Nonetheless, he looked forward to the telephone conversation he would later have with the editor. They had only
communicated by phone and through the letters they
occasionally exchanged. Blumenberg appreciated his conversations with this astute man, who was some decades
his junior. Speaking to him, he found someone at the
other end who was sufficiently sharp and well-read to

follow even his most obscure allusions, and clearly enjoyed adding his own anecdotes as soon as Blumenberg raised a topic. Naturally Blumenberg kept the upper hand in their conversations; he was responsible for the track on which it glided forwards and veered away from its respective course, but the man had enough confidence to approach him freely, not deferentially or, worse still, subserviently. For his part, the editor conveyed information and anecdotes from his newspaper world to the nocturnal Altenberge before they were published, and these were in turn commented on with relish by Blumenberg, who even filled the odd index card with them after the conversation was over.

Blumenberg valued this intense exchange, which took place purely via his ears in floating liberality. Their relationship remained unimpaired by the human, all too human aspects of close-range contact, in which skin and hair, clothes, smells, gestures, looks, irritating habits (while eating, for example) and many other things could have interfered. Blumenberg was not even entirely sure what the man looked like. He had once seen a small photo in a newspaper—the editor in a standing group, albeit with his head lowered and not very easy to make out. But that was at least twelve years ago.

Shortly before midnight it was time once again. He had taken a special bottle of Bordeaux from the cellar, a 1977 Saint-Émilion, a Grand Cru from Château Ausone, opened it and let it stand for a while, and now he poured himself a glass.

He took a sip: truly first-rate. The phone connection that day made the editor's voice sound a little distant. The conversation did not get going in as quick and uncomplicated a fashion as was usual between them.

It was because of him. Blumenberg had a burning desire to tell the editor about the lion; the wish was virtually blazing inside him. He desperately, truly desperately wanted to talk about it. One person had to at least hear about the lion, even at the risk of thinking him insane. Impossible. Even this special man on the nocturnal phone to whom Blumenberg felt connected in a completely natural way, would scarcely be able to deal with such an announcement. Being taken for a madman was the smallest danger; Blumenberg had to avoid pushing the editor at the other end into an awkward position. The irruption of the absolute could not be communicated. He would only have created confusion, which would in turn have had such an inhibiting effect on himself, Blumenberg, that they would both have been hopelessly stuck. Blumenberg saw the danger clearly, but constantly had to fight the longing to speak of the lion—now in particular, with the lion stretched out so invitingly and his mind overrun by words about lions.

Their conversation got going somewhat clumsily, and he emptied his glass of excellent wine out of sheer awkwardness. The weather in southern Germany: a devastating storm had descended on Mannheim, maybe that was still making the phone crackle; then the words began to flow more elegantly and they wandered from one topic to another. They spoke of Heidegger's childishly curved handwriting—he said the word 'curved' in a deliberately frivolous fashion—a hand writing that probably made a deep impression on the herd of Heideggerians because it belonged to the immediacy of the shepherd; Blumenberg spoke of the 'fur-clad herd of the onto-crank from the Black Forest', which must have seemed strange to the editor, but he merely laughed, and there was nothing unusual to be heard in his voice. They spoke of Heidegger's pseudo-radicalisms, the stagnations and dead ends in which philosophy was trapped time after time, and Blumenberg heard himself say in an unusually metallic voice that a hiatus would do philosophy some good, the sort of hiatus sometimes taken by large mammals. Gladly several years or decades, maybe entire centuries. As he spoke he glanced at the lion, which was looking over to him more purposefully than usual, though it seemed to him that the now-familiar flames of irony were flickering in its eyes.

'Let us put philosophy on ice for a while,' said Blumenberg, provoking slightly pained laughter at the other end.

The lion. Why did it never get up and wander about the study, not once so far? Why did it always lie in exactly the same place on the carpet, covering nineteen elephant feet, as if nailed to the floor, its head on the left as seen from the desk? He suddenly felt the urge to give the lion a sound kick in the rear to shake it up at last. That would overturn everything.

The lion bared its teeth, though it resembled a smile more than a threat.

Something had got into Blumenberg, and he almost compulsively spoke in abrupt shift about the dying Edmund Husserl, of how he lay in bed for an age, a man who had begun his philosophy with the observation of essences and concluded his life with, of all things, the observation of something no one would ever know about. 'Probably a lion,' he added in all seriousness, but the editor, thank God, either did not catch the last part properly or missed it entirely; at any rate, he did not react to it.

Then the conversation became muddled. They returned to the storm, then moved from the storm to the ghastly boredom of beach life, assuming one was not alone or swimming in the sea, then from beach life to the landing of British troops on the Falkland Islands, from the Falkland Islands to Maggie Thatcher, from Maggie Thatcher to Helmut Schmidt (the editor claimed to have discovered a secret sympathy between the two), and finally from Helmut Schmidt to the intricate problems of justice. It was hopeless to try solving them; politicians could not do it, though they constantly had to pretend they could, and it was not even the domain of philosophers. No philosopher in their right mind would presume to have an effective solution to even a single problem posed by justice.

There was a slight blemish in the fur on the lion's left ear, evidently an injury, that Blumenberg had not noticed before.

To take his mind off the lion, he spoke about his children. Children desired justice. They thirsted for it, more ardently and impetuously than adults. Yet when his children were young, he had quickly given up trying to pose as the just father. Any attempt to perform such a farce to them would have failed entirely; so he refrained from it. In doing so, he had trusted in the experience that some injustices would eventually redress themselves over an extended period. What had once been an advantage could develop into a disadvantage; on the other hand, a rejection that felt painfully unjust could—if sufficient time passed—yield a late reward.

The editor asked him if he felt like writing an opinion piece on his refusal to philosophize about good and evil in the moral sense.

'Definitely not.'

Blumenberg wondered for a moment why the editor, who surely knew him well enough by now to know that such a thing was completely out of the question, had even made the suggestion. The lion probably had something to do with it. The lion caused disturbances that the editor must have sensed over the telephone, without having the slightest inkling of who was in the philosopher's study, listening.

An opinion piece, so limited a space for a subject like that! He could not possibly explain why he refused to philosophize about good and evil in that format. He had always viewed Gnostic dualisms with suspicion; he had fought against them at all times. He had experienced absolute evil first-hand, yet he found the rigorous moralism, the waves of self-righteousness ridden by many students, insufferable. They all knew exactly who belonged to which camp, which led to grotesque misinterpretations in the case of someone like Ernst Jünger. Young people, who had not experienced that time, were not interested in hearing what *On the Marble Cliffs* meant back then, in 1939, when the book came out.

The young generation was full of revulsion and envy. His students had a vague idea of the threats hanging over their parents and grandparents and how pathetically they had behaved in the face of the risks. This filled them with revulsion towards that failure, and envy for the chance they had never been offered to gain certainty about themselves.

But he did not have the slightest inclination to roll out such topics or even touch on them, least of all in a newspaper piece.

He had been unusually vehement; the editor was probably wondering what he had done to deserve such a dressing-down. Blumenberg was normally at pains to express himself politely, tactfully and extremely cordially if he was unable to grant a request. His tone had been unduly harsh; he was sorry. Ruined. The conversation was thoroughly ruined because the one thing he was burning to discuss could not be mentioned.

Everything inside him urged, pushed, demanded, indeed almost screamed for him to finally, finally speak about the lion.

In a fit of melodrama normally foreign to him, Blumenberg was overcome by the feeling of missing, at that very moment, the only opportunity to discuss the monstrous thing that had happened and was still happening to him with a sharp-witted person who had a similar attitude to fundamental matters.

The frayed tassel of the lion's tail twitched slightly.

Getting by without witnesses was harder than he had thought. The nun—yes, yes, she was undoubtedly a proper witness, and an impressive one at that. Still, he would have loved to discuss the case with a scholarly mind who was familiar with the conclusive evidence left by the lion in the course of its appearances and disappearances over centuries, a man who was clever enough to speculate about it with him.

The lion had meanwhile laid down its head, quite as if the danger of becoming the topic of conversation had passed.

To defuse the abrupt shift in tone, Blumenberg asked after the editor's work in an emphatically friendly manner. He could tell from the humoristic descriptions of how many piles of useless books were lying on his desk, and how many colleagues were constantly bursting into his office to pester him with silly questions, that the editor did not hold it against him.

They said goodbye. His study, illuminated by three lamps in the midst of night, had him back.

The phone call had left a bleak emptiness inside him. He felt like a sucked egg. For the moment, he did not know what to do. His productive zeal, the immense diligence that had always distinguished him—it was all a battle against emptiness. A battle that could not be won, as he secretly knew, a defensive spell like the singing of children in the dark woods.

He thought of his own children again, of the light in their rooms that he had sometimes switched on in the night. Decades ago, when they were all still little, he and his protruding ears had been responsible for taking care of pains that occasionally assailed the children in their beds. He could still feel the children's despair when they were tormented by insomnia or haunted by nightmares. In those early days he had succeeded in playing the comforter. Now the lion comforted him, but the pact of silence that had come with it was difficult to keep. Furthermore, the lion gradually seemed to be losing some of its consoling power. Why had it not made an appearance at today's lecture? A warning sign! It annoyed Blumenberg that he was already so dependent on his lion that he became flustered in its absence.

No, he would not publish anything about good and evil, least of all something directly relating to National Socialism. He had also abstained when Hannah Arendt made her theory of the banality of evil public. Perhaps he would not have judged it as harshly in 1963 as he did now, though the book already displeased him then. Her theory may have been correct on some points, but using the Eichmann case to demonstrate it, at the neuralgic moment of his trial in Israel, when the state's founda- tion—to which people like Eichmann had indirectly contributed—was still relatively recent and Eichmann was the only target, the only available culprit whom the Jews had been able to secure; to trivialize this man of all people through the banality of evil was a mistake, in fact more than that, it was reprehensible. Six million dead had moved to the new state. The problem was not whether it was permissible to call something 'evil', but when and how. She had no understanding of the power of symbols. What bothered him most of all were her brash tone and her ambition to stand out with as bold a theory as possible.

Sigmund Freud's *Moses and Monotheism* had also been published at a problematic time. Freud's portrayal of Moses as an Egyptian came in a year of extreme distress. The Jews, who had little choice but to cling to their his- tory, were now having their greatest patriarch of survival, the historical hero of the exodus, taken away from them and handed to the Egyptians. To be sure, Freud's intention had not been destructive; what he wanted was more to lift some of the burden of being special off the Jews to lessen the hatred that surrounded them in Europe. But that was precisely the mistake. A truth that might have had a liberating effect a few decades earlier or a few decades later was not appropriate at such a time.

It was a grave error to think that the truth would set us free, no matter when, no matter where, no matter by whom it was uttered. Everything depended on the time when a truth could be dealt with and when it could not; if made public at the wrong time or in the wrong place, it would only cause confusion and defiant rejection. The truth was fulfilled over time; via long diversions and deviations, it gradually came to light. Germany was a perfect example: much of what could only be uncovered little by little, and still caused distress on occasions, would only have caused a mass collapse of the fragile support structures of life if it had been revealed directly after the war. Forgetting was necessary. Without the healing effect of forgetting, the new state could not have civilized itself.

And anyway: truth. Could the truth-seeker trust that the existent would simply open itself up to them? Or was there violence involved, trickery, coercion, a mortifying interrogation of the object? Was the capacity of humans for truth tied to the economy of their needs or inspired by their talent for happiness, their talent for craving abundance guided by the idea of a *visio beatifica*?

Perhaps it was the realization of never being in possession of the truth, in fact, that set us free and came closest to the truth, in stark contrast with the promise that possessing the truth set us free.

Blumenberg was now quite doped; he took his glass off a typescript and gave himself a refill. He wanted to dispel the subject, but it kept forcing its way back. The crimes of the Wehrmacht: a textbook example. In so far as the crimes were committed by the simple soldiers and middle ranks, not only the few generals sentenced in Nuremberg, it was still difficult to speak about them in public. It would require many members of a generation dead, or that the few who were still alive had become too decrepit and lacking in influence to harm society any more.

In his agitated state, normal work was out of the question. He rose abruptly and walked in a curve around the lion, almost tripping and losing his balance; but the lion lay there unperturbed, as if it knew very well that no fall was to be feared.

Blumenberg went over to the music room to calm himself with a recording of the *Goldberg Variations*.

The music, which had, after all, originally been written for a sleepless man who had requested a work of gentle and lively character to cheer him up, did indeed calm and relax him. Good, evil, evil, good—the tiresome subject gradually moved to the background. Gould's fingers were hammering on his entire body with precise haste, and as he began to feel pleasantly tenderized, other thoughts took hold of him.

He thought of a portfolio, a very particular black corrugated portfolio with the inscription 'What is the very last thing?'. He kept his dying sketches in it. In a rather light, witty tone, not put on paper with any heaviness, the portfolio contained his fantasies about the way people died. People he knew personally and figures familiar from public life—a speculation about their final hour, which had not yet come at the time of writing. The when and the how, the hopes they may have entertained, ailments that plagued them, relief that came, turbulences that confronted them, expectations that remained unfulfilled, or were fulfilled so comprehensively that they led to terror. He imagined, for example, a likeable young jackanapes who had studied with him as an ancient, more then hundred-year-old man going up to Adonai, who whispered the answer to the question of his existence in his ear so that the angels would not grow jealous. In the face of the many, many adepts of eternity around him, the man had but a single wish: 'Please erase my existence.' At first glance, it seemed weightier than intended. The tone was somewhat akin to a fizzy glass of aspirin.

He had been collecting such speculations for years, and they secretly gave him a morbid enjoyment. Perhaps he would return to his study later and begin a sketch about how the editor, that clever arch-sceptic, died.

A Further Interlude, in which the Narrator Moves Time Along by One Year

Despite having promised otherwise, the narrator will now speak out again. We are in May again, but May 1983 rather than May 1982. What happened in the world between those dates? No doubt millions of times more than one narrator, however, conscientious, could (and should) commit to paper. We recall: Helmut Schmidt had to hand government affairs over to Helmut Kohl. The Argentines, who had plunged into war with flowery words of nationalism, got a bloody nose on the Falkland Islands. The Iron Lady chalked up the victory and stayed in power. Ronald Reagan was the American president. Klaus Barbie, the Butcher of Lyon, was arrested in Bolivia. *Stern* published the bogus diaries of Adolf Hitler. Things got quieter for Dietmar Schönherr and Vivi Bach. Ingrid Bergmann and Glenn Gould died, as well as Walter Spahrbier, the smiling, horn-rimmed-glasses-wearing bringer of good luck from West German TV, who had always appeared in a high, black peaked cap with a shining post horn insignia on the front.

Gerhard was lonely. He had not only lost his girlfriend but also Richard, the ever-morose, but occasionally very amusing Richard, who seemed to be gradually changing into a different person abroad. His letters, which reached Münster at increasingly long intervals from Argentinia, Bolivia and Peru, testified more and more to a gift of self-immersed observation that Gerhard had never known in him. Foreign life had evidently assailed him to such a degree that there was no air left for his usual whinging and smart-aleckry. Gerhard missed him a great deal, and was particularly curious about the transformed Richard, who was possibly less sleepy, less of a drunk and less fixated on his ancient stories. Did Richard write such clever letters to his parents in Paderborn too? Gerhard did not find a replacement in Hansi; Hansi remained the same as always—unapproachable, aloof and intrusive as usual with his recitation tic. There were no further rapprochements; they greeted each other from a distance with a nod, and that was that.

And Blumenberg?

Blumenberg had not come one bit closer to the lion phenomenon during that whole year. Superficially speaking. Or if he did, then at least no breath of the innermost secrets coursing through Blumenberg and the lion had reached the narrator's ears. A narrator does not initially see; they hear and transform what is heard into images, or listen with their eyes—'To hear with eyes belongs to love's fine wit', as one of Shakespeare's sonnets so fittingly puts it. On one occasion, the narrator had a sense from the rummaging in the study and the thoughts rising to the ceiling—though it was only a suspicion, nothing more—that Blumenberg kept a secret portfolio containing everything he wrote about his lion; miraculous germinations, scribbled down hastily, very hastily, not typed as usual or written in the clear hand that dwelt in roundness. Everything about himself and the lion. The portfolio was hidden; evidently there were no right hands for it to fall into. And the narrator's ear was not sharp enough to guess where the portfolio was kept, not sharp enough for the hear-saying, for the say-hearing, for 'the listening never stops', and so the eye could not focus enough to recognize what lay within.

Blumenberg also collected lion notes in conventional form that did not need to be hidden, however, and the index cards in question had swelled into a substantial pile. The lion had barely appeared in the lectures, but lay in the study on its traditional carpet as it always had. Habituation inevitably set in; sometimes it happened that Blumenberg simply forgot about his lion during the night. Everything stayed as it was. Blumenberg had not risked a physical approach. The lion still exuded strength and assurance, perhaps not as intensely as at the beginning, but steadily, with the result that Blumenberg even slept better and more restfully, when he actually slept, and sleeping pills, which had always been his last resort to sleep at all, were no longer necessary.

Richard

May was not very rainy that year. He was only soaked by lukewarm rain once a day, then fanned dry by lukewarm breezes. Richard had already been travelling through the southern part of the American continent for months. Opulent novels in which life veritably spilled forth from every page, in which levitations were as natural as the base activities on the earth, had lured him here, probably the last stirrings of revolutionary fever that had once seized him, the son of a senior postal clerk in Paderborn who worked in the administrative service, at high school, but, above all, the distrust he felt towards his criminal native country—a malignant, ever-smouldering distrust whose edges flickered with paranoia.

He had failed, thoroughly so, but failure no longer had his body and his thoughts under its control. Richard had spent months more vegetating than alive, with nothing in his head except his failure. Outwardly he had displayed a jaded manner, fallen asleep in lectures and picked up women in pubs as a wickedly alcoholized specimen who could perhaps only be saved in bed. He had even behaved superiorly towards his friend Gerhard, had to put on his act for Gerhard of all people, that good old soul. He, Richard, had seen everything there was to see—what a laugh! In reality his failure had paralysed him, and he had not lived at all; and Gerhard, whom he had always chuckled at and picked on a little bit, had secretly been an object of envy.

'I'm a total failure,' Richard said to himself or, rather, said it very gently into the airstream, and the airstream carried it to the birds crossing above; he found it amusing, for his failure had now become lighter than a feather. He had been lying in a hammock for days, no, for weeks; he could no longer keep track of the rushing herd of days. The hammock was located at the bow of a little Brazilian freighter sailing along the whole never-ending Amazon River.

He had never been able to impress his professor in Münster—Münster, that nest, had meanwhile shrunk into a little toy town in Richard's mind, something a four-year-old could reach into and go 'brumm brumm' with his car—with anything, anything at all. The scenes proving that now presented themselves to Richard's inner eye in perfect illumination and focus. He saw himself as a pale worm creeping along behind the professor—a skewed image, for the professor had always rushed home, into his own realm, too quickly for Richard or whoever else to creep along behind him. Nonetheless, Richard's wormlike nature was true to life, and sometimes this worm that Richard had long been raised its head pleadingly: 'Please,

please, Mr Blumenberg, could the professor please notice me.' Richard laughed as he recalled his comically fruitless efforts to leave a meaningful sign of himself before the implacable eyes of the professor.

The months he had spent in South America so far, in Argentina and Chile, had meanwhile softened the contempt he felt for his own country. The fact that things were calm and comfortable in Germany, while Pinochet had come to power years before in a bloody coup and his neighbour General Videla had ruled as an iron-hard dictator who had political opponents snatched off the street, tortured and thrown in the sea, gave him pause. He had come into contact with the horror that seeped from these dictatorships as soon as he became more closely acquainted with people and their fear. He felt a gradual suspicion towards the moral rigorism of his own generation, their obstinate belligerence towards their parents, an attitude with little interest in knowing what it was really like to live under fascism. And he began to understand why this rigorism had to get on the professor's nerves, even though he had never voiced it directly, at most, in hints only understood by those who wanted to understand.

Sailing about in the middle of the Amazon, lying in a hammock while the warm breeze stroked his body, in this special position which made his body feel happy as never before, Richard was able to remember clearly everything that had tormented him in the last few years, but his clarified misery no longer hurt; the mild breeze carried it away. Even Isa, whom he had despised with all his being, now appeared in a different light: she had been a failure too, and alarmingly similar to him in that respect.

So where had he failed? With his dissertation. He had spent two years turning it around in his fingers but never managed to get beyond page eighty-six. The very thought of it was enough to silence his laughter, but the whole thing was laughable nonetheless, almost silly, as Richard admitted to himself—totally silly, in fact, this fruitless pondering over every page to assess whether the professor would like it. But no, of course the professor would never like such a miserably composed and sloppily conceived page; he would be too disgusted to read it at all. That was roughly how Richard had imagined the professor while reading, or rather not reading, a page of his dissertation and the professor's disgust, imagined in every possible variation, had prevented him from embarking on page eighty-seven, and after it pages eighty-eight, eighty-nine and so on.

It was over, thank God. The subject had not been to blame. Or had it? Was the topic too big for Richard's mind? Too subtle for his crude character? Perhaps the intricate relationships between the disciples and their master and between the students and their professor—both disciples and students as essences to be illuminated, flesh that had to be infused with spirit—had prevented him from simply grabbing the subject between his fists and getting cracking?

Already as a child, Richard had been profoundly impressed by the outpouring of the Holy Spirit, especially the little flames that leapt onto the heads of those gathered. When his grandmother told him the story again and again, as he had requested, little Richard always reached into his water-combed parting in expectation of a little flame, but to his disappointment it never proved willing to stray in that direction.

That childlike inflamedness, which could not be regained by the adult Richard, or at most with a caricaturing grin, was of little use to him for his dissertation. Nor was it any use to him that the young Richard had always understood the glib Parthians to be one or more Pantherans, though that did make matters very exciting, for Richard would have loved to speak to a fully grown panther. No, Richard had failed because he had proved unable to confront the biblical texts with cryptic Blumenbergian questions and shoot accurate answers onto the paper as if bouncing shots off the cushion in a high-class game of billiards.

It was only the chapter on the Pentecostal singing of water birds in the village of Ringelai, in the Bavarian Forest, that Richard considered passable, perhaps even cunning; and maybe also the footnote about various medieval Jewish communities in which it was the custom to place the little children on the synagogue's lectern at Shavuot when they were around five years old, then carry them to their lessons, where they learnt the first Hebrew letters and were fed with sweets, as the Tora was supposed to enter them sweetly. All well and good, but he had not, of course, been able to show Blumenberg these individual elements separately from the other, laborious parts that never got off the ground intellectually. Laboriously, yes, he had gone back and forth laboriously between the Old and New Testaments, had dutifully started with Moses and proceeded via the Book of Ruth to Joel, to the Acts of the Apostles, to John, had dutifully explained how the miracle of Pentecost had redressed the building of the Tower of Babel; but he did it with the intellectual dreariness of a Bible mechanic, and not even a good one, until the ordeal had come to a halt on that accursed page eighty-six.

How he had toiled to find out everything about the Medes, the Parthians, the Elamites and the Cyrenians, who had chatted in such lively fashion with the Egyptians and Romans after the miraculous illumination of the flesh, each speaking in their own tongue yet immediately understood by all the others. But what Blumenberg had casually demonstrated to his students from each lecture to the next had remained beyond Richard's powers: looking from a thing to something else in order to reach an insight into it rather than a vague monotony.

Then he had inherited money from his grandmother and made the decision to spend a year in South America. He had decided to sail along the entire long Amazon River, though starting not with the Amazon but the Ucayali, one of its main tributaries. And now he was finally on the Amazon.

Grandmother's money had been converted into traveller's cheques and dollars, which he carried on his person in a special zipped pouch made of cotton cloth. His actual travel bag had seen better days. Its reddish embroideries had meanwhile become scuffed and grey, various seams had burst, and the handles were falling apart. Nonetheless, he was proud of the thing. A curious shepherdess was bending over a sleeping shepherd—on the front. On the back, the shepherdess had fallen asleep herself. The bag made him feel like a travelling hero from some glorious epoch who had nothing whatsoever in common with the other tourists out there.

His arrival in the tropical world—now that had been a real adventure. He had landed late in the evening at the small airport of Pucallpa, named after a Peruvian *capitán*. The moment he set foot on the little stairs to leave the propeller plane, the humid tropical night placed itself around his body like a suffocating cloth. The first breaths were unaccustomedly thick and warm. Millions of insects swarmed around the lights that were mounted on scaffolds on the roof of the reception hall and illuminated the runway from high above. There was a buzzing and a sizzling in the air, a sizzling accompanied by tiny wads of smoke, produced by insects burning up on the hot lights. Richard knew that unimaginable masses of insects lived in the tropics, and now he saw such masses for the first time in the glaring artificial light of a tropical night, finding it both fascinating and alarming.

He took a liking to the hotel immediately. One entered through swinging doors like those in an American saloon. He felt like a cowboy when he heard his footsteps creaking on the wooden floor and placed his precious bag on a stool next to the reception, which was also a bar. Tired characters were hanging around and playing dominoes; they barely raised their heads to look at him. There were no doubt some cockroaches, but they were evidently too shy to show themselves when he switched on the light in his room. A tall, dark bed from colonial days awaited him, and the obligatory mosquito net hung from the ceiling.

For breakfast there was a buttery cassava porridge with fried bananas, along with an ebony-black coffee in a speckled greyish-white tin cup that he immediately became fond of; he would have loved to attach it to his bag with a piece of string. When the saloon doors swung open he saw low rows of houses and above them a leaden blue sky, hanging low and interspersed with red dust clouds, he saw whirling gusts of wind that stirred up the dust of the trodden clay paths. The hotel was located on the tarred main road which led down to the river.

Cargo boats were moored on the riverbank. At the loading area, half-naked porters were carrying baskets and bulging sacks on their shoulders, loading and unloading the ships in two orderly marching columns; between them were teeming passengers who were pushing their way into the boats or had just disembarked. At the sight of all this, Richard could not help being reminded of Hollywood films in which Roman or Egyptian slaves carried out the business of the toilsome and the burdened— though the clothes were usually white in those films, while the little that was worn by these men shone in every colour. The men were also smaller and stockier. Indios from the Peruvian jungle worked hard on the banks of the Ucayali.

Before giving himself up to the great river, Richard wanted to explore the distributaries of the Ucayali. To that end he struck a deal with the owner of a wooden boat, who agreed to row him about. And so, the following day, he had the pleasure of a little trip that went through river bends, past little forests of Algarrobo trees, past dead waters that smelt rotten and were covered in a fleshy green layer of plants, as if momentous secrets had to be concealed beneath them. Boats were stuck in some of the dead foliage, abandoned by their owners. Perhaps the boaters had been suffocated by the plants and were telling their desperately sad tales down there in disembodied voices, more murmuring than speaking.

Butterflies escaped from dreams fluttered towards him, gigantic sluggish gliders coloured azure, crimson and flaming orange, or tiny ones chequered in lemon-yellow and apple-green. A dense cloud of mosquitoes accompanied the boat; they did not seem to harm the ferryman but they stung Richard's flesh mercilessly, even though he had rubbed himself amply with an appropriate ointment and smelt revolting, by no means inviting. The ferryman was someone who observed quietly, refraining from all commentary when Richard flailed about like a madman to chase away the pests until he finally resigned himself to his fate. The squelching and water-hopping of little animals, jumping off water lilies and floating palm leaves, accompanied their journey. These waters seemed to be veritably seething with bugs. They lived and squelched and gurgled, they flew, swam and hopped on and on. Crocodiles, however, which he had hoped to see, stayed in hiding. Instead, the murmuring silence was broken by the squawking of parrots: flocks of annoyed birds with green-blue bibs rose from the trees.

In the night, Richard lay in bed with swollen red legs, a scratched neck and scratched forearms, cursing, tossing and turning, scratching and scratching yet more, even though he had forbidden himself from doing so a hundred times. He did not get a wink of sleep. In the morning, a battered western hero sat over his cassava porridge, doubting whether he should really undertake the great river trip.

A few hours later he was lying in the hammock of a small freighter headed for Iquitos. No, it was not comfortable. It was hell. The hammocks were strung up very close to one another and he failed to secure a place on the deck, so he was now lying bottom to bottom with a complete stranger; the toilets were so filthy that he resolved to stop eating and drinking. Once his horror at the imposition of such unaccustomed physical intimacy had given way to a fatalistic placidity, good neighbourly relations were established; they passed around bananas and flat bread and played cards, laughed and chatted.

Richard had learnt his Spanish in Argentina, and some of the expressions he used caused the others amusement.

The faces of his two hammock neighbours, stocky middle-aged merchants on their way to the market towns along the river with sacks full of beans and sweet potatoes, became serious as soon as they asked Richard about Germany. Germany filled them with respect. They had never heard about the division into East and West. They considered Hitler a great man, a real *cojudo* with balls like a bull who took no nonsense; one of them even thought the dictator was still alive. Despite the warm relationships that developed from hammock to hammock, Richard was glad when they arrived in Iquitos a few days later and he could enjoy the comfort of a bath, in a hotel that had been the extravagant domicile of a rubber baron decades earlier.

Two days later, after exploring the little town—which had sprung up like a mushroom because of the rubber trade and quickly faded again—he was finally on the river that began as the Amazon right there at the confluence of the Ucayali and the Marañón. Things could not have turned out better: on a Brazilian freighter, whose sky-blue exterior and green superstructure had already appealed to him at the docks, he managed to secure the front hammock. There he now lay alone outdoors, letting the mild breeze stroke his body. The wind was just strong enough to prevent the mosquitoes from resisting, and too weak to become unpleasant in the long run. What paradise! When he concentrated on what he saw in front of him he could imagine that he was all alone on the ship, and that this ship was navigating as if by itself according to his wishes.

The Amazon was pervaded by a monotonous fogginess, interrupted only by dramatic sunsets and mild sunrises, and Richard enjoyed the uniformly passing days, which demanded nothing, absolutely nothing of him.

He knew from the jungle stories he had greedily read that at certain points the Amazon widened like the sea, and that was exactly how it was, except that Richard was looking at a brown-grey sea rather than a blue one; the shore was mostly out of sight. Then it came closer, and the Amazon resembled a river once more. It was a mighty river; the Amazon left no doubt about that. Whole trees floated on it, carried away like matchsticks.

Days had become weeks, weeks had become a month and more—Richard had long since lost track of the passing calendar days. Spending one similar day after another in a hammock, more comfortable than anything else in the world, put him in a peculiar state of limbo. Close to the shore, far from the shore, his thoughts sailed along in perfect freedom; he alternated between dozing and waking, saw the moon, the stars, revelled in the clouds that covered the moon and revealed it again, and saw these phenomena with such intensity that it seemed as if there were some secret correspondence between his own comfortably safe body and the celestial powers. It was just as the professor had once said—as a child, one was truly granted the world's favour; the world had once been there for the child so completely that it bowed to him, wept with him and escorted him on all his journeys.

But Richard, delicate Richard with his fine blonde hair, had soon lost the world's favour and had shifted to a state in which he hated his parents and did not really know what to do with himself. And this wretched ignorance had accompanied him for years, until one day he told his professor about it with glazed eyes in the hope that he might reveal to him his purpose in the world, but the professor did not perceive his need in the slightest; he had probably only registered his existence in some distant corner of his memory. The pitiful Richard, who drowned his sorrows more and more in alcohol, had now become a meaningful being drifting along the centre line of the earth, having equally fluid mental conversations with the dead and the glib panthers of his childhood.

He felt he had been moved into happiness. The weather was mild and warm, never hot or blazing; sometimes a warm rain fell on him, which he enjoyed as much as the subsequent drying off. The sunrises and sunsets were spectacular. In the evening, tongues of red fire glowed above a compact black mass of forest, and in the morning a rosé-coloured early mist cloaked the shyly emerging, delicate woods in a negligee. What astounded him most was how suddenly the chorus of frogs and toads entered. The last rays of the sun had barely retreated from the water before the chorus let rip within a split second. Loud! Thousands of frog throats croaked and creaked like there was no tomorrow for several minutes, and as abruptly as the noise had broken out there was silence again, mitigated only by the familiar sound of the ship's engine.

Everything unpleasant moved far into the distance. Germany, that crampy little country with its crampy politicians, crampy terrorists and crampy feminists, was simply comical—a little country that took itself very seriously, that was all it was. The captain contributed to Richard's good spirits with a generous supply of marijuana, and by generally being a very pleasant associate. It was easy to communicate with him: Richard spoke his Argentine Spanish and the captain answered in a Spanish-Portuguese hotchpotch to which he gave interpretative emphasis by rolling his eyes, furrowing his brow and using his nimble hands to draw in the air.

Richard did nothing and simply lay there, not even feeling up to reading, which had always been his source of comfort; *Being and Time* slumbered in the depths of his bag. In the morning he awoke with a great plan that was carried by the indifferent river into a floating approximation and dissolved into a thousand little glittering drops, which was no great loss, for Richard awoke the following morning with another equally splendid plan.

Nocturnal Encounter

One evening in the twilight the freighter steered towards the shore, even though there was no settlement to be seen from a distance. But lo and behold, there was a landing stage. The frog noise had just faded with the last rays of the sun, and birds flew up from the trees, some of which protruded deep into the water. Now Richard could make out a small settlement, not solid houses but a mixture of huts and log cabins, most of them perched on poles. The captain indicated to him that they would have to spend the night there; he did not say why, but insisted that everything had been taken care of and Richard could sleep in one of the huts.

It was a lumberjack settlement. Half-naked porters climbed on deck over a thin plank and loaded sacks onto their shoulders, then headed back again in an orderly marching column whose heavy steps made the plank bend precariously far. A few carbide lamps were already burning in the settlement. There were whites and Indians, and Indian women were cooking on open fires. The captain showed Richard to a small hut that also stood on poles. A young girl who was not entirely trustworthy as far as the cleanness of her fingernails was concerned served him the food on a tin plate, beans with a bit of meat, and also handed him, with a shy smile, some water and a black coffee in a tin cup. The smile still floated about in the hut long after the girl had gone, and Richard caught himself repeatedly smiling back, albeit only at the wooden wall, which was decorated with pictures of bathing beauties from a magazine.

He decided to take an evening walk, which led him around the settlement for the duration of a cigarette; he could not make out much, as it was already dark and the few lamps only illuminated the entrances to the huts. The water close to the shore was full of black lumps—the last water birds, heading for their sleeping nests. When he arrived back at his hut, he heard rumbling from above. A blackish ape figure was sitting on the roof flailing its long arms, which Richard took as an invitation to join it on the roof. Something pulled at his trousers from behind; when he turned around, he was more than a little shocked to find an anteater in front of him, climbing up him by digging its front claws into Richard's trousers and using its long snout to search the pockets, folds and cavities of his clothes. Richard soon noticed that the anteater was friendly, but he still found it unnerving to be subjected to a body search by an animal he had never encountered before. It abruptly turned away from him and went off into the night. The ape had also disappeared. Baffled,

Richard crushed the cigarette in the sand with the tip of his shoe and ascended the little steps to his hut.

He counted himself lucky that he there was a hammock there and he didn't have to sleep on the ground. A mosquito net was fastened to a hook in the ceiling, and one could spread it out around the hammock like a tent. He put out the light and lay down. No longer used to lying in an enclosed space, he took forever to fall asleep; he missed the ship's movement, the humming of the engine and the breeze.

Something whooshed underneath him; it had to be under the floor of the hut, between the poles. Richard listened with his ears pricked—there: the whooshing came again. An animal prowled around, bending branches in the process. At the same time there were strange calls from the distance that he could not identify. The whooshing could be heard at irregular intervals. To calm himself, Richard had to give a name and a shape to the animal that had chosen the space under the hut as the base from which it went out into the night and kept returning. He resorted to the speaking panther of his childhood, though it was sneaking around silently at the moment because it missed the Medes, Elamites and Cyrenians, but perhaps Richard could start a little conversation with it if he leaned out of his hammock and addressed the squatting panther through the slits in the floor?

Far, far away, rising from strange depths yet nearby, he heard a sound that went right through him. Dark, as if blown from a horn, sometimes weaker and sometimes stronger, a threat moving towards him from the night, perhaps halted in its progress by thick tree trunks that deflected the sound slightly away from his hut, but then making directly for him again with undiminished strength. Something unimaginably horrific for which he knew no name was coming to get him. Sweat broke out from every pore, and he felt his hands trembling. He lay alone in the darkness of the night with his eyes wide open, unable to stand up and light the lamp. He suddenly remembered a dream from his childhood from which he had awoken screaming every time: a shepherd came to a peaceful mountain village of wooden houses with snow-covered roofs leading a herd of mammoths, enormous animals, each one of them bigger than the houses they passed on their trail. The shepherd was tiny next to them, as were his two sheepdogs. Then the smallest mammoth, which had been walking at the end of the line, fell over and lay in the snow. The shepherd swore and kicked its belly with his boots, but that did nothing to get it up. He ordered the dogs to attack, and they bit into its fur all over; but the bites had no effect because the dogs were so small. Then the shepherd flew into a rage and took out a whip, seemingly from nowhere, with which he thrashed one of the dogs so mercilessly that he broke its spine. The deafening cries of the dog filled the valley and the ears of young Richard, who then awoke screaming loudly.

Although something inside him knew that the scene had emerged from his memory, it took a hold on him as if he had just dreamt it again—with one difference: the largest of the mammoths, an enormous, shaggy brown animal, turned its head towards him and looked at him with its little eyes; then it raised its head with the long, curved tusks up high, and the terrible sound it made, as if blown from a horn, echoed through the valley.

The panther still had to be lying down there. Richard clung to the thought that the speaking animal could rescue him, so he leaned his dream-clouded head out of the hammock and sought to make contact.

At first there was no movement, not even the whooshing. But when Richard pleadingly whispered down to the panther a second time, a dark, yet clearly intelligible voice reached his ears with the words: 'I am listening.'

Richard held his breath for two or three seconds, then a rushing filled his head and the words came flooding out. Everything that had ever burdened him, everything he had ever wanted to know, why was he there, where had he come from, where was he destined to go, why suffer —guilty, innocent, punished, unpunished or saved, by whom, why, what for—everything, everything, everything came out, and from below he heard laughter that sounded a little grumpy; but once he got going, Richard was unstoppable, and confided the whole jumble of his worries and questions in the slit in the floor. And lo and behold, in the course of the night, which lasted a small eternity, things were put in order: natural history, human history and theodicy. The questions were substantial and the answers were precise and as sharp as fangs; the conversation ended with the panther's cryptic words that the jungle would soon cease to be a jungle, Richard would see.

When the conversation came to a halt, Richard leaned back in his hammock. Before sleep carried him away, however, another scene fluttered about in his head, leading him to the hallways of the university in Münster, where Richard opened the door to Blumenberg's office. Without much ado, he sat down opposite the professor at his desk and got started. The professor's eyes grew wider and wider, they displayed amazement; with this splendid image in his mind, Richard went back to sleep as morning broke, slept more deeply and blissfully then he had ever slept before.

The day's activities had long started when he awoke. For breakfast he had the usual buttered cassava porridge, this time brought by a white-haired woman whose mouth was one great wrinkle. The freighter was only set to disembark around noon, so Richard still had time for a walk. He followed a wide path leading out of the settlement and had only been walking five minutes when he found himself looking at an open field, big, enormous in fact, and fairly square-shaped, a bare surface that had been cut into the woods. There were no young shoots on the surface, only sand and some meagre grass. The sight of it was disturbing. All the powers he had collected during the night were now taken away from him. Richard turned around and had only one wish: back in the hammock and on with the journey!

Manaus

As soon as he was lying where he wanted to again, his mood lightened up. Drifting along in the tepid breeze, he found it easy to relive the nocturnal adventure; it seemed precious, more and more precious, as the fear that had originally accompanied it was gone.

A girl had contributed to his shimmering state of mind. Fourteen years old at most, and so beautiful that Richard sometimes had to close his eyes because he could not believe that such a beautiful person even existed. They had become acquainted when the girl went to the ship's bow to look at the churning water. Before long, she spoke to him, he would never have dared. With a motion so natural that no one could have had the slightest objection, she pulled up an unused stool and sat down next to his hammock. Richard sat up a little; he suddenly felt like a patient in a hospital bed, with a nurse next to him watching him closely.

It all began so easily. Richard didn't have to do anything. María came several times a day, sometimes even after dark, and kept him company. She was evidently travelling without companions. He had never encountered a being with whom he had such a genial and effortless rapport. All the gearwheels that normally started moving inside him when he encountered an attractive woman stayed still; he felt no urge to boast or perform one of his usual comedy routines. He simply waited until she came, was happy when she came and felt blessed with every meeting, as if a slender goddess had visited him to drizzle dewdrops on his forehead.

Of course, she was still very, very young. But had Novalis not desired a very young girl, and had the hunchbacked Lichtenberg not found happiness with a girl decades younger than himself? The age difference between them was not so great. Eleven, twelve years at most, maybe thirteen. That was also significantly less than the difference between Humbert Humbert and Lolita. The advantage of his Lolita was also that she was not some petulant, tacky middle-class girl from the American north; and he, in turn, had not used any of Humbert Humbert's shady strategies to get close to her. He could not find anything shameful in their burgeoning relationship, and made no attempt, none whatsoever, to touch María. She had already given him a parting kiss on the forehead several times.

She was Brazilian, and enjoyed teaching him words in her soft language, which Richard patiently repeated like a good pupil. The graceful way she emphasized the words with gazes from her large, serious eyes and underlined their meaning with eager little fingers was simply enchanting. Oh yes, he was in love—in a chimerical way that demanded nothing, absolutely nothing of him, as a perfect passivity kept him in his hammock.

And yet plans gradually formed inside him; he could not refrain from weighing up ways and possibilities in his mind that would enable him to take María to Europe. It was difficult to enjoy his happiness in the knowledge that it would soon come to an end. She already felt like such a natural part of his life—impossible to think of never seeing her again; this was also a painful reminder that he would not be able to spend the coming years in a hammock, nor probably in Brazil. As soon as his planning took on more specific character and his imagination began to demand direct action, he felt unease. At the thought of introducing María to his parents in Paderborn, the rousing spirits that had inspired him disappeared again.

As he found out, María's family lived in Belém and an aunt of hers in Manaus. She would disembark with him in Manaus. The town on the Rio Negro, the place from which Fitzcarraldo had set off on his crazy naval adventure, exerted a stronger pull on him than any other city in Brazil. How things would continue there with him and María was anybody's guess. The last days in his hammock passed in quiet melancholy and with quiet fears.

When they left the Amazon to travel up the Rio Negro for a few kilometres, the ship became restless. People gathered their belongings together or stood at the railing chatting loudly. It was time. His bag was quickly packed.

When the freighter arrived in Manaus and he found himself forced to stand on his legs again, he noticed how close the beautiful is to the terrible. The city vomited its rubbish down the embankment and into the river. People were crawling all over the rubbish. María had offered to accompany him to a hotel; he wanted to look for one in the city centre, near the Teatro Amazonas and the Palácio da Justiça. But he was not getting away that easily: the captain gave him a spirited farewell. They were the last passengers to leave the ship.

What was awaiting him at the docks alarmed him. Once the usual crowds had dispersed a little, he saw people squatting around, sitting on little boards with wheels, standing on crutches, stricken with horrendous diseases, with boils and maimed limbs; it was such a blood-curdling sight that Richard had to avert his eyes. God knows he had travelled through many poor countries by that time; he had witnessed Bolivian farmhands being treated coarsely by the Argentines at the border, like animals, kicked and sprayed—veritably drenched—with DDT for disinfection purposes. He had spent hours on the backs of trucks with Bolivian market women who carried sacks so heavy that he could not even lift them, but they did; and he had seen an old beggar woman die in the Avenida Monroe, where he had lived in Buenos Aires. But the misery that confronted him here was more garish. María, who did not understand why he was standing there helplessly, tugged at his sleeve and led him away. In his confusion, he did not even notice the famous Mercado, a building constructed on an iron frame designed by Gustave Eiffel that now served as an indoor market.

On the walk away from the docks, he became a little calmer. Further inside, once they had left behind the decrepit shacks and a few crude new buildings, the city became more and more impressive. It was not very difficult to find a passable hotel; he even found an appealing one whose foundations shone with the floral tiles used by the Portuguese to decorate their rich houses. In the tropical climate, tiles probably formed a more durable exterior than wood or ordinary plaster.

María promised to drop by the following afternoon and show him around the city. At the moment, everything was too new for him to worry about whether she would return or not. He was very happy with his hotel room; it had a balcony supported by an iron frame, with a view on a square-shaped plaza with two mighty palm trees. Nonetheless, he felt captured in his room, which was stuffy. After a few minutes he went outside to sit in front of a cafe and feel at home in the open air of Manaus.

Though he was no great fan of opera, he would have loved to attend a performance at the Teatro Amazonas—the mere thought of listening to an opera in a small town in the middle of the jungle was exciting—but the famous theatre, built in 1896, was closed. Its interior, including the opulent ballroom, was evidently quite dilapidated and termite-infested; there had not been any glamorous performances in decades.

In the evening he went to a small restaurant and ate a feijoada made with black beans, slices of hot peppery sausage and a ton of garlic. After that he drank too many caipirinhas, which did not agree with him. He roamed the streets for a little while, feeling more and more abandoned, and finally lay in bed quite early with a heavy stomach, unable to sleep. More out of desperation than inclination, he took *Being and Time* out of his bag, opened it to a later chapter—he had struggled several times to get through the beginning, and barely understood a word— whose title allowed him to relate it to his own situation: 'The Fundamental Disposition of Anxiety as an Eminent Disclosedness of Dasein'. His eyes came to rest on a passage that seemed apt, a passage which stated that 'the flight of Dasein is flight from itself', but that 'in the object of this flight, Dasein comes up directly behind itself.' Richard let the book fall on his chest—there was undoubtedly something coming up behind him, something deeply frightening was coming after him. But the fear was diffuse. As Heidegger put it, 'Nothing which is ready-to-hand or present-at-hand within the world functions as that about which anxiety was anxious. Here the innerworldly totality of involvements of the ready-to-hand and the present-at-hand is of no consequence to anxiety; it collapses into itself.'

He had sunk deep into his sagging bed. He had lugged *Being and Time* along in the hope that in differently coloured countries, under a sun that glowed differently, the meaning of the enigmatic book would reveal itself almost of its own accord. This plan had not succeeded thus far, and so he had carried around the heaviest part of his baggage like a useless rock. Now, for the first time, a passage in this book had grabbed him, spoken to him, as if it had been written especially for him. Something came out of the book and ascended into the uncanny. He felt evil mental fingers touching his heart.

After a hard night in which the dark meal of beans entered a sinister alliance with his fears, he awoke completely exhausted the next morning. Five past ten. The weather was the same as always. Damp. Warm. Friendly.

He felt like going to the famous water lilies on the other side of the blackish river with María. In a guidebook he had seen the giant round leaves like drinks trays, so large and strong that a thin little lad could safely doze inside one without sinking. Air-filled cells allowed the *Victoria amazonica* to survive while floating. Indentations on its raised edge let the rainwater drain away. Perhaps the water lilies would give hints to him and María about their shared fate. Nature, so full of miracles, could reveal the probable in the improbable—who knew, maybe they would feel the urge to live on one of the leaves.

He spent the morning roaming about. The city was starting to grow on him. The Portuguese colonial buildings were exceptional, filigree and opulent at the same time. What wastefulness in the middle of the jungle! It must have been an incredible effort to transport all the building material over there. At the time, there was no industry in Manaus that could have provided the material for such extravagant constructions.

He waited for María on the hotel veranda, full of worries as to what should be said and done, conceiving plans only to discard them immediately. To realize them, he would have had to grow far beyond his limits. They would have demanded the vigour of a giant.

María came on time, which was remarkable for a South American. The people usually came at least thirty minutes after the agreed time.

She seemed inhibited, not greeting him with the same elegance with which she had placed a hand on his forehead or taken his hand before. She is probably as trapped as I am, Richard thought. They walked together somewhat stiffly for a while; Richard overcame his hesitance and made his 'water lily' suggestion, which was met with a brief nod of agreement.

Richard was surprised. Normally would have responded to such a suggested with delightful chatter and immediately taught him new words relating to the water lily; today she was remarkably taciturn.

She was half a step ahead of him and walking to the harbour, but taking a different route from the one they had come by. Richard had not taken his street map with him, as María was leading him. The surroundings became increasingly impoverished; all around, he saw low houses with half-crumbled annexes whose garish paint was peeling off.

Richard stopped in astonishment. There was a yard with pieces of meat hanging on the washing line. Salted meat drying in the sun, María assured him; evidently a speciality of the region he had never heard of. The hanging meat seemed macabre to him, and he felt no great desire to try whatever meal it was used for in the near future. Because of the rain the meat had to be watched over and repeatedly taken down and hung up again.

Her aunt lived not far from there, María told him, adding that she was sure to know a good boatman who could take them there. They turned a corner; the usual bustling of people going about their business was absent here, and the street seemed poverty-stricken. Two young men were leaning against a wooden wall, their hands tucked under their armpits. Richard began to feel uneasy and would rather have switched to the other side of the street, but he trusted María, who surely knew her way around there. She stayed one step behind him—Why is she staying behind? he thought, she should be going ahead—and then the men stepped forwards from the wall and went up to him. A stocky fellow, smaller than Richard, wearing dark trousers and a dark shirt, with sunglasses on his broad nose, started speaking to him. Richard did not understand; it sounded like a stream of abuse, with the man barking the words out at him. He turned to María for help, but she had retreated further and seemed somehow absent. Then the other one got involved too, pushing him in chest aggressively, a bigger man in a Hawaiian shirt with a golden cross on a chain dangling in front of his chest—'María', he kept hearing the name; evidently these characters knew the girl and wanted payment. But what for?

Richard tried to appease them with a few Spanish sentences, but that had the opposite effect: they became even angrier, though it was as if they had rehearsed their anger at the theatre. Richard almost found their enraged voices amusing; he touched the arm of the man in the Hawaiian shirt to calm him down, but he was pushed into the shed, and before he knew it he was lying on the dirty floor surrounded by all sorts of junk.

He had scraped his hands through the fall. The palms were burning. I'll get septicaemia, he thought. Then the man in the Hawaiian shirt was standing over him, fingering around at his hips. Richard was overcome by anger. He wasn't going to surrender so pitifully in front of his girl, not like that. He gave the man a sound kick, sending him stumbling backwards, and Richard got back on his feet. He was wheezing and sweating. In front of the open gate of the shed stood María, surrounded by light, her feet pointing inwards and her hands pressed together under her stomach. He did not have much time to reflect on this sight: the stocky man in black ran towards him and rammed a knife into his heart. Where did the sunglasses go? thought Richard as he saw the face with the meaty nose so unfathomably close to him. The look on it was not angry so much as methodical and professional.

Richard fell to his knees, and his hands felt that his belly was covered in blood. He looked out of the open gate for as long as he could; his girl was standing in the glaring light. Had she? He struggled against the thought and tipped sideways.

Addenda

It took almost two months before Richard's parents in Paderborn learnt that their son had died in Manaus. His body had been found quickly, robbed and with no papers. The passport only turned up six months later in a rubbish dump. The hotel already reported a missing guest the day after it happened, but the man in question had written his name in an illegible scrawl and the porter had neglected to retain his passport, meaning that the name could not be established with certainty. The police found the first clue in a heavy book lying open on the bedside table in his hotel room: 'Richard P.' was written in a school-boyish hand on the flyleaf. Only after a few weeks was it finally confirmed that the murdered man was a young man from Germany by the name of Richard Pettersen. His killer was never found.

When his father arrived in Manaus to bring his son's body to Germany, he was met with an unpleasant surprise: it was nowhere to be found. It had probably been buried somewhere along with other corpses that had long remained unidentified.

Hermann Pettersen had to endure much hardship and bitterness; without a word of Portuguese and only poor English, and with half-hearted support from the German embassy, he rushed for days from one government office to another, only to be fobbed off with confusing and evasive statements about what exactly had happened to his son and where his body might be. He had to fly home without a coffin.

In Münster, word of Richard's death only got out half a year later. He had given up his flat, and none of his friends or fellow students were in direct contact with Richard's parents. The newspapers did not report the murder. The news spread by chance through an old school friend of Richard's who had moved to Münster for her studies. Gerhard had been wondering why he had not received any letters from his friend for so long; until then they had arrived at increasingly long intervals, but still with a certain regularity.

So now Gerhard had lost Richard forever too. That caused him to work more strictly than before. Münster was ruined for him; he wanted to get away as quickly as possible. Two years later he had already moved to Munich, started his first assistant post and met a local woman who became his wife not long afterwards.

Hansi's path was more complicated. It too led away from Münster—first to Zurich, then Berlin, alternating several times between the two cities, then to Berlin for good. He did not finish his studies at any of the universities where he attended lectures. He did cause something of a stir in Berlin, however, when he opened a philosophical consultancy in Bleibtreustrasse, near the Kurfürstendamm, taking out large newspaper adverts with chopped up Blumenberg quotations. 'What is a suitable résumé on one's deathbed? Make provisions now!' read one slogan, while another claimed: 'Every person affirms themselves by passing certain tests and founders upon failing them. I can show you how to fail better!'

His fellow students in Münster had, incidentally, been right in their suspicions: Hansi was wealthy and could do as he pleased. His urge to recite had dwindled over the years; as long as he had his consultancy, where he usually sat in a whitewashed treatment room waiting, he was no longer seen going from one cafe to the next with his poems and the dented tin ashtray. Drawn in by his clever advertisements, a few curious people had actually visited his office; they were received ceremoniously and seated in a Wassily chair, but even the craziest ones never went back. Hansi was and would always be a loner. Incapable of listening to people, he could only talk them down from his desk; he seldom looked at his patients while speaking, but rather at an acrylic painting on the wall facing him that depicted a swimmer diving into the water. Hardly anyone who strayed there in search of advice, and had to pay a hundred marks after being subjected to an hour's worth of invective, would stand such treatment a second time.

But Hansi's old urge returned at once when his office closed down. He no longer went up to restaurant tables with poems, however, but with self-penned tracts, which made the guests hate him even more quickly than the poems had. He dispensed with the ashtray. He evidently found it wrong to demand money in public when he wasn't offering an aesthetic performance, but rather his own calls to reason.

So time passed, and Gerhard's prediction proved accurate—perhaps not the cheek twitch, but everything else. Hansi's decline took place with alarming speed. After a few years, the dapper Hansi of former days who used to haunt the restaurants of Kreuzberg and Charlottenburg was no more: Hansi had gone to the dogs. A trained observer might have noticed that his clothes had once been of high quality; now they were scuffed and dirty. He still wore his hair long, even though it was prematurely grey and thinning. With his striking features he almost looked like Antonin Artaud in his later stages of decline, as missing teeth had made his mouth collapse.

When the Wall fell, Hansi worked himself up into a frenzy: so many new people wandering about aimlessly, in need of awakening!

In 1991, one late Thursday afternoon in October, when the bustle at Zoo station was especially great, he took up position down in the hall, in front of the stairs leading to the trains. A few minutes later he fixed his gaze on the passers-by, who rushed past without paying him any attention. More out of habit than need, he took a bit of paper from his trouser pocket and raised his voice. Hansi had never had a sonorous voice, and he now made a great effort to be heard in the high-ceilinged hall, which ended in shrieking. With tensed neck tendons, he urged the passers-by to return to themselves.

'You are surrounded by a desert of sadness!' he shouted at the people, of whom only a few looked at him and even fewer slowed their pace. They thought some drunken hooligan was yelling at them.

'Clueless!' the words erupted forth, 'You are clueless, cluelessly you gaze on the pale ruins of your repulsive lives! You in your holes. Out, in, holes everywhere. Dirthole! Dirthole! I would not take your holes as gifts. You will die in your holes. In its hole every beetle is the sultan, say the Egyptians. The Egyptians are wise. But you are beetles! You do not want to leave your holes.'

Wagging his forefinger, he gesticulated wildly: 'To be on the safe side, you will now all be declared dead and removed from the area of operations!'

He placed his finger against his forehead as if having to think for a moment, and his voice grew quieter and lower: 'In Africa, the expressive are beautiful. Whoever rolls their eyes most expressively and can tremble most impressively with their chin. Girls grab a man like that out of the group with their arms swinging loose. Whoever can tremble with their chin wins! Come to me, I say! Chosen ones, come to me!'

Once again his forefinger went up in the air, and once again he started shrieking: 'The person who confuses themselves and others is the ordinary person. The common herd. You are the most ordinary people. Dirthole!'

Now his voice was shaking with boiling anger, and the finger he held out at the people shook too: 'But I know how to stop you from continuing your dirtying like ordinary people. The one who stands before you is the chosen one!'

He stood on tiptoe, then firmly on his feet again. 'Here'—he pointed at his feet with a jerky movement—'here stands One! One, the One! Hansjörg Cäsar Bitzer. Removal from the area of operations has been decreed! Out! Arseholes out!'

Hansi was now waving his arms about as if shooing flies away, then he assumed his usual threatening pose: but first he opened his case. 'The LORD has worked! Lambs will emerge from my briefcase, and anyone who thinks of the Lamb of Christ is not wrong! Anyone whose chin trembles as I open the locks is not wrong. Come on, you arseholes! Just believe that things will soon be over for you. You will marvel at my lambs. I have lambs with me, unique sacrificial lambs only waiting to run between your legs. Behold, I raise my forefinger as Christ once raised his forefinger at the Last Supper'—but Hansi only raised his finger briefly, then leapt at a passer-by, snatched his bottle of Coca-Cola and threw it on the ground, where it shattered and its contents spilled out—'You there, you will betray me, and you, and you, and you, you will all betray me! Traitors will all be removed from the area of operations!'

The young man was too startled to do anything about Hansi. Because the madman's behaviour and the words he was screaming were simply too bizarre, a few curious people had turned up in the meantime: an elderly couple, a child and a group of young Poles. The woman had cocked her head to hear him better. They watched Hansi from a good distance. Then two guards from a private security firm came from behind and grabbed him under his arms with trained, irresistible hands. He desperately attempted to defend himself, turning his neck around wildly, screaming, thrashing around and kicking the security men in the shins; his powers of resistance grew with every step. While the men dragged him towards the exit, he screamed time and again for his briefcase and his lambs. He screamed, 'It is I, I am the stone that screams!'

'Lambs!' The word filled the hall while Hansi collapsed between the two. They thought it was a trick and carefully let his motionless body slide to the floor. They pushed him, shook his chest and then called the paramedics, men in bright jackets who started working on him, but all they could do was establish the man's death. When the briefcase was opened, it was found empty. That is, not quite—a picture postcard with a painting by Zurbarán was stuck to the bottom. It depicted a bound lamb, heart-rending in its innocence, the delicate ring of a halo above its submissive head.

So many deaths of relatively young people. Some will object that the narrator would have done better to refrain from presenting such an accumulation, especially in this bookkeeper-like manner, without examining the time that had passed and framing the deaths in an intricate web of allusive connections. It is a narrator's duty, however, to report even the improbable truthfully. As briefly as possible. So people simply died in the story, and it was simply recorded—recorded for purposes of new transformation, as will soon become clear.

But first another death must be added. Not a premature one, but one in keeping with the person's age: not twitching about, but quietly in her bed (though not with her hands folded, for as soon as the nuns standing around the bed attempted to bring her hands together, they moved apart again), her tiny coifless head propped up by a bulging pillow, Käthe Mehliss died on 12 March 1987 with the words: 'I'll start again in a minute, wait and see!' Even then, she still found the strength to articulate the 's' exaggeratedly sharply, as had always been her way.

A final doubt must be voiced: we hesitate to invoke Wittgenstein's claim that each of these deaths was worth a whole life. Were they? The opposite could equally well be true—death has no value, but life has all value.

The Lion V

Over the years, Blumenberg had grown used to his lion. His life had become lonely after retirement. He rarely left the house, he lost contact with his old university, and no longer had anything to do with the bustle of academic activity, from which he had already largely withdrawn before retiring. He had only remained in contact with his own family, and the intimacy of his coexistence with the lion had intensified. They lived together like an old married couple. Words were unnecessary; they understood each other without them. At the same time, their interaction became somewhat lax. A sloppiness crept in through an alternation of forgetting, overlooking and re-noticing. The sheer delight, the rousing of flurries of ideas once triggered in him by the lion, was absent.

The lion too had its moods, and Blumenberg was subtly attuned to them. Sometimes it would have a morose night and sleep with its head turned away from the desk, and not a hair on its body moved. Then Blumenberg struggled in vain to stir more vitality in his lion with a torrent of words. The Egyptians claimed that the lion was stronger than sleep and always awake; that was hardly true of his lion. His lion was provocatively sleepy for long periods of the night. Perhaps the Egyptians had other means at their disposal for keeping their lion companions in an attentive state.

He had long since developed the habit of speaking to it like an old friend—he could laconically call things like 'Oh come on! Don't make such a fuss!' down to it when it was refusing to pay attention to him again. Blumenberg could tell from the way the tail twitched whether it was a nervous, impatient reaction or whether the lion, by dragging the tassel of its tail slowly across the carpet, was indicating agreement. In rare cases, a growling sound was heard from the depths of the lion's stomach, something between a sigh and a grunt, to which Blumenberg replied: 'Ahh! Dissatisfied again, my precious comrade!' He called the lion a 'master of inconspicuous expression', or—adapting a statement Nietzsche made about himself—a 'clown of sleepy eternities'.

In time, however, there were many nights in which Blumenberg completely forgot his lion. In early September 1994, the lion disappeared for a whole night for the first time. Blumenberg felt a burning agitation in his chest. He constantly paced around his table and the high desk. He could set about reading a book or a newspaper, he could switch on the TV—nothing helped. His eyes kept scanning the windows to see if the lion would perhaps come in from the garden. If he heard rustling outside he opened the door, which immediately struck him as absurd. When the lion was there, he forgot about it. When the lion was gone, he felt robbed—more than that, he felt threatened.

In bed the oppressive chest pains became worse. His head also hurt, and he felt nauseous. He got into as fearful a state as if the catastrophe of his youth had caught up with him afresh. After sinking into deep unconsciousness, he was admitted to hospital the following day.

By the time he was allowed to return home, something irrevocable had happened: the frailty of the final days had come over him. Even the lion could not change that. It did please Blumenberg that the lion lay there so quietly again during the first night in the study; but it was a shaky pleasure. If he had only had the strength to stand up, he would have gone over to the lion and bent over to stroke its fur with his hand. Blumenberg was now exceedingly eager to finally touch his lion, but the mere thought of having to bend down and possibly collapsing over the lion kept him in his working chair. Trembling with weakness, he sat there like a prisoner. The lion, three metres away, was no longer enough to calm him. Without intimate, tangible contact he had little to counteract this paralysed, ominous staring at death. He saw himself as defeated, and could draw no consolation from the fact that real, true history was always at the feet of the defeated who had death in their sight. The subtle theological overtones that characterized his work, and which the lion's make-believe existence seemed to affirm, were of little help now, even with one eye on this tremendous witness—he was unable to believe honestly that one was not simply dead when one died.

Some nights he fell into deep despair. It was all in vain. He had worked so hard for nothing. Soon there would be no one left who read his books. They would be forgotten. He recalled some of his proud former claims, for example, that he would not abandon his life's work until the last line was on paper. He now found such pronouncements inflated. The disappearance of his public intellectual presence had begun. He was not yet dead and already no longer existed.

Things that had required no effort in the past now also remained unmastered, for example, pulling one of the stacked boxes out of the shelf to get to old recordings and picture material he had collected. He wanted to find the image of two lions striking a tree of life with their paws, but could not get out the box in question. Instead he found an old cigar box with a dried-up Brasil, the kind he had smoked in the 1950s. He closed the lid.

For the most part, work was now out of the question. Writing a letter cost him a great deal of strength. Even the phone conversations with his beloved editor, which he had once so enjoyed, were now only rarely possible; he found it too tiring to concentrate. And the editor also seemed to notice that he was unwell, which was in turn an agonizing burden on the conversation for Blumenberg. Some of his old strength did return at times in subsequent months, allowing him to take up his work in the usual fashion, but that refreshed state did not last long. He knew that his remaining time was short.

On 28 March 1996 his wife found him lying dead in his bed. There was a trace of lion's smell in the room, but it was so slight that neither the distressed woman nor the doctor who had been summoned noticed it. An opened pack of Cailler chocolate had slipped from the dead man's hand. There was a little piece of tin foil on the floor. On Blumenberg's pyjama shirt and the bedspread there were short, dull, yellowish hairs that could hardly have come from a human head. They remained undetected amid the busy bustle around the deceased. The death notices that were later sent out were adorned with postage stamps of the Lion of Lübeck.

Inside the Cave

'Abode,' Samuel Beckett wrote, 'where lost bodies roam each searching for its lost one. Vast enough for search to be in vain. Narrow enough for flight to be in vain.' Beckett had a cylindrical container in mind. Closed at the top. No escape. Not so high, only sixteen metres. A different container must now appear in the reader's head, though it adopts important objects, sonic utterances and gestures from Beckett's 'lost one': for example, ladders; for example, in attenuated form, the wheezing; for example, the oblivious, slowed-down play of fingers—a large space, changeably large and larger, no space of captivity, at least not a narrow one, with a high ceiling and secondary spaces branching off unforeseeably from the main space. Light. Sometimes weak, sometimes stronger, light, possibly coming from all sides, light, as if controlled by the eye of the beholder within the cave, but an insistently unchanging light, even if only a glimmer, from the narrow cave exit, albeit coming from a great distance, hard to make out for tired existences, hard to reach. Quiet in here. So quiet that a single sound leaps out of the silence as if etched into it. Like a drop breaking the flat mirror of a cave lake. But it is impossible to hear the world aging, despite the sharp urgency with which every sound becomes audible.

The cave's dress is also changeable. A changeable wall on which images gather. Sometimes a naked cave wall, sometimes animated by flashing apparitions, sometimes hung with tapestries from which individual figures can step forwards or leap forwards—for example the partridge, before being received into the tapestry again when no longer needed and staying there in its quiet, partridge-like way until another emergence is desired. Ladders on the walls, likewise at changeable points. But, as far as can be seen in the main room, not currently in use.

If one did not know that the main space could also change its shape, one would say that six figures are placed comfortably in the middle of the room. Some on an old, slightly ragged Chesterfield sofa, some on the floor leaning on pillows and piles of covers. One leaning against the belly of a mighty lion, mighty also compared to the humans, who seem small next to it: the lion, the eye-catcher of the cave.

Never before had Blumenberg rested so peacefully. A dubious claim; Blumenberg's memories of previous resting states had paled far too much for him to be capable of comparing them now. The lion's breathing communicated itself to his back. The lion exuded warmth; a breathing radiator enclosed him from behind. The lion's smell, spreading an untameable animal presence, pungent but not unpleasant, wrapped itself around him.

A *when* formed inside Blumenberg. Thinking went more slowly here than it usually had before. He had not found it hard *when*—but when? What? Where did this *when* lead? He could no longer estimate the time that had passed, could no longer arrange the actions it contained in a logical sequence. It was as if caverns that functioned according to unknown principles had opened up in the logical space of his thought. His inability did not disconcert him, and hence the *when* disappeared.

He opened his eyes as if for the first time and saw five people gathered around him, of whom he recognized two. Two of the names immediately came to him: Käthe Mehliss and Gerhard Baur. Baur, whom he still remembered from the meeting in his office, even though this meeting was now far away, as if someone else had conducted it, far away, as if he had merely resided for a fugitive moment in the mind of this other man who had once been a professor.

However short their encounter may have been, Käthe Mehliss had stuck in his mind. Here too she was wearing her white coif, which emphasized her head, but she seemed younger than he remembered her, while the other four people, Gerhard Baur too, looked older. The girl who had always sat in the front row did not appear quite so young any more; the two men, who had presumably been his students too and whom he remembered only vaguely, were likewise middle-aged.

Blumenberg closed his eyes and surrendered himself to the cosy warmth of the lion. When he stretched out his right arm and lifted it, he could place it on the lion's left shoulder. Everything was permitted. The lion was there only for him. Blumenberg felt sure that the lion would have allowed him to climb onto its back and ride it like a child. The lion would tolerate him burying his face in its mane; he was probably even allowed to reach between its jaws and touch its teeth, just as he had once poked his forefinger behind his little Axel's front canines to tease him a little.

His eyelids fell shut. Immaterial lids guarded immaterial eyes, yet if the will was there, he could see more intensely with them than with normal ones. No reason to speak or attempt to make anything happen. Then he felt a small movement near his left hand, or was it a scraping? He opened his eyes: the partridge had returned to—to what? Converse with him? Blumenberg gently placed it on his lap and carefully stroked its head with his forefinger. Although this contact was an uncannily convincing illusion, there was pleasure in stroking that smooth-feathered head while the partridge turned its head towards him and looked at him with one completely round, gleaming black eye.

'I was mistaken about Antonello da Messina's picture of the study,' Blumenberg said, 'of course it's not a quail perched on the parapet, it's you.'

The partridge nodded.

The memory of his study suddenly returned with surprising clarity. 'Forgive me, I didn't have a copy of the picture on my desk, and it had been a long time since I last looked at it. You are in the picture, and it was to you, you alone, that Saint John bent down. He played with you, happy as a child.'

The partridge nodded.

'Oblivious to his surroundings, freed from the task of remaining in contemplation of God, the man of God tickled you under your beak. I don't suppose you want to tell me what you were talking about back then?'

The partridge aired its feathers with a shudder and made a quiet beating sound with them.

'He would have spoken like a simple-minded child— ga-ga, goo-goo, gi-gi,' said Mehliss. She had barely lost any of her upright, sharp manner. She was sitting very straight on a pile of blankets, her opaquely stockinged legs with black patent leather shoes crossed: 'And the partridge will simply have done what partridges do: chirp!'

The partridge crouched down on Blumenberg's lap.

Richard had one hand raised far above his head. His bent fingers clawed at something in the air in slow motion. 'I used to tell my tomcat bedtime stories and take it to bed as soon as my mother left the room. A fat, lazy, black fellow. Or maybe it wasn't mother; maybe grandmother.'

He had sunk deep into the Chesterfield sofa next to Isa, half lying and half sitting, and the hand he raised at the end of his long arm was the only indication that he was taller than Isa.

'I used to enjoy eating partridge,' Blumenberg said, 'but now that I have you so close to me that's inconceivable, as inconceivable as if no partridges had ever been eaten.'

The partridge shuddered on his lap.

'It is the ghastly way of the world that people shot them—admire, paint, shoot, deign to speak to them, shoot and so on and so forth,' said something that was perhaps the partridge. The voice sounded astonishingly deep for such a small bird; but every word was gasped out as if the animal's vocal tools, especially its little tongue, were struggling to replicate the human voice.

'I never ate chickens, not once,' Isa said. 'Maybe as a child. But that changed at sixteen, when I saw the inside of a poultry fattening farm in Brittany.' She was surprised that this poultry fattening farm, the dampness of the hall, came to mind so clearly. She paused for a moment to check that what she had just said was true.

'Some kind of poison had been mixed into the chicken feed to make their feathers fall out. They were all bald. All injured. Thousands of chickens in a warehouse, the air cloudy from the dirt that was being kicked up. It was unbearably hot in there. And the clucking every-where—but in waves, not individually. After that it was impossible for me ever to eat another chicken.'

'Well,' said Blumenberg, 'so young people can be overwhelmed by strange sights, and are evidently capable of making a choice.'

'But that's not true,' said Gerhard, 'I cooked a stewing hen in your flat once, and you liked the soup so much that you gobbled it up like anything.'

Isa turned away from Gerhard, who was sitting to her left very much on his own, his long legs in the middle of a mountain of cushions.

Hansi struck a match, an action that drew attention through its excessive loudness, with a tiny explosion that turned into hissing and crackling. His cigarette was shaped like a real cigarette, and it glowed as he took a puff, but it was a skilled illusion, just like the lips pinched around it. The smoke that rose as he exhaled was not swept away by any gust of wind, only by emptiness; it was artful, a curly, serpentine construct that slowly unwound itself, as if each waft of smoke released and untied a knot inside Hansi.

Hansi was leaning against the sofa in unusually casual proximity to human beings, between Richard's and Isa's legs, and he put his head far back while smoking. The back of Isa's hand was touching his hair, which was lying on the seat cushions—if one could still call it hair, this hair made of spindly grey shadow threads. Hansi was silent, and seemed to enjoy his silence.

'What we did or didn't eat does not count here,' said Mehliss. 'There's no eating here, at any rate.'

'But the suffering that humans have caused us certainly does count,' the partridge pointed out. It had puffed itself up and was trying to look dignified, but was in danger of choking on its own clucking as a result.

'We're not here to chew on old jeremiads,' said Mehliss. 'That is not the purpose of our stay here.'

A quiet wheezing was heard.

'What would the purpose be? The great breath of life?' asked Hansi, who was so intensely preoccupied with the latest expulsion of a smoke cloud that he had no interest in a possible response. The cloud departed horizontally, in waves.

'I cannot believe in my personal resurrection, for the haptic, the undoubtedly haptic, is gone.' Hansi put his head back even further, closed his eyes and mumbled: 'My anger at the world is also gone. Without my anger at the world, I am hardly more than the bit of simulated smoke that enters me and exits my throat. I am simply unable to summon up the anger again.'

'Knowing something about everything while not possessing anything takes some getting used to.' That was Mehliss.

'Well, I don't see anyone here who feels the urge to run up against the cave walls or climb up a ladder to find somewhere to slip through further above,' said Gerhard, 'though maybe it would be very easy; our container doesn't strike me as very solid-walled.'

'The closed space permits the dominance of wishes,' Blumenberg mumbled faintly.

'But the suffering that humans have caused us certainly does count.' The voice rumbling in the partridge obstinately insisted on its chosen point. 'Humans always imagine that they are the only ones to suffer.'

'Quite right,' Blumenberg replied somewhat more animatedly, 'that is the world superstition of their distinction. They suffer and imagine that they were superior to other creatures. They are unstoppable in their anthropocentric vanity.'

'Over there, in the darkness, the potato sprouts grow several metres long,' said Isa, pointing to an approximate area further back. 'It's eerie.'

The old cave encouraged the emergence of unsound structures. 'Place of false fertility, place of deceptive nutritiousness,' said Blumenberg. 'But we are in a new cave, where the Platonic promises are no more convincing than in the old one.'

'There's no eating here, no potato sprouts,' observed Mehliss. 'Here the sprouts are weeded.'

Gerhard objected, saying there was no sign that they were being fed with the flesh of Leviathan for the purpose of carnonization. Perhaps they were not righteous enough. But he was not keen to sample such fare anyway.

His eyes, like those of the others, were focused on Blumenberg, as if they were hoping he would provide the important insights. But Blumenberg's eyelids had dropped again, his scholarly urge for interpretation lost. He lacked the tiny bit of gusto for a precise consideration of the lives lived between there and here, that drive of concern which is required even for subtle distinctions. And the others did not demand any further statements from him. Each one lost themselves, each strolled about in a waking state scattered with dusky sleep particles. Only the sharp-eyed Mehliss seemed slightly more awake than the others. There was a diabolical sheen to her black patent-leather shoes.

The partridge had meanwhile slid off Blumenberg's lap, stalked a few steps further and got lost in the vagueness, coming to rest in the tapestry.

'But we are'—Richard hesitated and once more used his fingers to take hold of the air of a thought—'we are still thirsty in mind. In Brazil I once saw a sloth that . . .' His words came to a halt and he could not continue.

'To adapt Epicurus,' Gerhard said, 'we are entangled in endless dialogues, perhaps not Greek ones, and perhaps not divine ones. So far removed from concern that we entangle ourselves purely for the sake of entanglement and tell each other stories we have not suffered.'

'It would be better to keep silent about those we have suffered,' said Mehliss.

Isa lifted her head and looked on both sides. 'What we have suffered is sitting up on the ladders, looking mockingly down at us. My white dress is sitting up there doing flapping things.'

'Flapping things?' said Gerhard in surprise.

'Wiping motions.'

'The privilege of the weak to tell stories,' Blumenberg mumbled to himself.

Richard raised his right hand for a change, then his left, and bent his fingers in succession as if counting: 'All debts added, all debts subtracted.'

'Perhaps something would be gained if each of us tried to capture the rest of what happened upon their death,' said Mehliss. 'I remember how dry the bedclothes feel when one strokes them.'

'Sweetie, sweetie, sweetie-pie,' said Isa.

'We—we are floating in a peculiar limbo between salvation and guilt.' Richard's hands sought to imitate a weighing motion: 'To—to—but we would have to wake up for that.'

He said nothing for a while, then continued: 'Was it a Frenchman? A famous Frenchman, who said that remembering means one has stepped out of the uncertainty of awakening, and there is an angel floating somewhere up there that brings the recovered world to a halt?' His hands came down again and he thought of his old embroidered bag, the bag, which he pressed to his chest with an urgent movement, even if nothing was left of it but a cushion made of air.

'Flesh shell,' said Mehliss.

'Ascents from the dungeon of the flesh,' said Isa.

Blumenberg opened his eyes again. In the distance, faintly, he heard signals—a whistling. No, his memory did not offer any notion of where the whistling might have come from, nor any images of the wreath floating in the sea and the urn at the centre of the wreath sinking into the water, an elegant urn of hardened salt that soon dissolved in the sea. Nor could he recognize that the sounds came from a captain's whistle and corresponded to the melody played for a captain who died aboard his ship and was buried at sea.

Hansi smoked and smoked. He was searching through his thoughts for the image of the lamb in his briefcase—was the word 'briefcase'? Briefcase, yes, it was a briefcase. He saw the animal's front and rear hooves lying bound on the plinth, saw the lamb's wool, airy like little clouds, its dark downward gaze, but the artist's name eluded him. A Spaniard? Fleming? Italian? Soon there was not one bound lamb lying there but herds of lambs from promised lands, from villages, settled around hills, going past him. The muzzle of a cow approached as if it wanted to lick his face with its tongue.

Words faded. Names faded.

Gerhard looked affectionately at the open hand on his lap, as if it held the golden cup.

Isa sat bolt upright. 'The potato sprouts are creeping closer and devouring our names.'

'There are no sprouts here. Nothing is devoured here. I still have everything gathered under my coif,' responded

Mehliss. The sheen on her patent leather shoes vanished, proving she had lied. When she attempted to recall her favourite cantata, she had forgotten one word—

> Adam must in us decay,
> for the new man to be saved
> Who is created in—
> —in whose, in what image?

She furrowed her brow while the rest of the words effortlessly returned:

> You must rise in spirit
> and leave the grave of sins,
> if you are a member of Christ.

But she was not going to give up so easily. She quietly tried to hum the text, but could still not find the missing word. She swayed her head incredulously; everything was so confusing, much too confusing to grasp.

What was left of Blumenberg's presence of mind gradually became duller. Images and half sentences drifted past him in torrents, washing individual words away; he realized with quiet terror what important things were being washed away when he noticed that he could no longer remember his name, nor the names of the others sitting near him. Words crossed inside him like passing flocks of birds, fell and rose, darted overhead; he fingered about on the words' bodies, which he briefly managed to grasp, attempted combinations of syllables, but to no avail.

'What was the name again?'—with vague hope he thought that if he could remember someone else's name, his own would also come to him; but the *again* had already snatched the name away. Even the woman's coifed head, which had always inspired clear words in him, that head, which was swaying back and forth inexplicably slowly, which he observed with a residue of inquisitiveness, did not do its duty.

And yet, at least one name came to mind again: Goethe. And a few lines immediately swept past him:

(You) gloom-embraced will lie no more,
By the flickering shades obscured,
But are seized by new desire,
To a higher union lured—

He, who had previously been leaning slumped against the lion's belly, moved his back away, put the soles of his feet on the ground and got to his knees, where he stretched out his legs above the joints, lifted his upper body and touched the expanse with trembling arms.

The lion had also risen. Its fur gleamed in the light. The muscles bulged, showing who was in charge.

With a majestic, a majestically resounding sound, 'Blumenberg!' shot forth from the lion's maw. Until then, the man in the cave had been little more than air in the air, yet the calling of his name seemed to fill him with other matter. Irradiant blood flowed through his veins. He shone and trembled, holding his shaking arms outstretched. And then the lion swiped its paw at his chest, tearing him into another world.

Acknowledgements

Bettina Blumenberg provided astute and liberal help from the beginning. She showed generous respect for an outsider's view of her father, wittily accompanying me in my tentative attempts.

I was encouraged by conversations and correspondence with Michael Bernhart, Ursula Flügler, Friedhelm Herborth, Michel Krüger, Dietrich Leube, Ernst Osterkamp, Klaus Reichert, Claudia Schmölders, Hermann Wallmann and Uwe Wolff. A number of them gave me access to material, especially Michael Bernhart and Uwe Wolff. Thanks are due also to my editor Julia Ketterer.

Any attempts to find correct Blumenberg quotations will be in vain. I have, however, adopted half sentences, short phrases, modified trains of thought and individual words from the revered philosopher. Wherever he might be now, I salute him and ask him to bear with me.

Sibylle Lewitscharoff